Justine
and
The Story
of O

Guido Crepax

EVERGREEN

EVERGREEN is an imprint of Benedikt Taschen Verlag GmbH

© for this edition: 2000 Benedikt Taschen Verlag GmbH
Hohenzollernring 53, D–50672 Köln
© Guido Crepax
© introduction: Paolo Caneppele and Günter Krenn
Translation (introduction): Chris Miller, Oxford
Design: Lambert & Lambert, Düsseldorf

Printed in Germany
ISBN 3–8228–6302–5

CONTENTS

Infinite Distance In Close-Up

"Justine" and "The Story of O"
as seen by Guido Crepax

PAOLO CANEPPELE
GÜNTER KRENN

Some things never change. Even today, self-confessed readers of the Marquis de Sade are few and far between, though his books are everywhere; as Jules Janin wrote in 1834, they are hidden in every library so carefully that anyone can find them. In 1834, Donatien-Alphonse-François de Sade had been dead for twenty years; in fact, he had already enjoyed two decades of immortality. Today, we can admire the prescience of Guillaume Apollinaire, who, early in the 20th century, announced that Sade, considered a nullity throughout the 19th century, might prove a master in the next.

The life and work of Sade have so often been analysed and interpreted, that any brief summary is in danger of reinforcing the hoary chestnuts of tradition. In the field of debauch, he had imagined whatever was imaginable, but by his own confession, he had accomplished much less in reality. Defining himself as a libertine, he insisted that he was neither a criminal nor a murderer. This is a point fundamental to our understanding of Sade's rather picturesque personality: his transcription of the imaginary was unconfined, and he sought to live out his needs and desires in the worlds of fantasy and imagination.

"The World as Desire and Imagination": many of Sade's excesses can only be understood as a reaction to his social environment and historical circumstances. Several of his contemporaries acted as he did, though few have attained a similar level of popularity. For Simone de Beauvoir, the contemporaneity of Sade lies in the way that he unsettles the reader by forcing him to problematise the very fundamental question of human relations. In certain respects, Sade's writings – like those of Voltaire, which antedate them by several decades – can be seen as a satirical response to Leibniz's theory of the "best of all possible worlds"; the function of those protagonists of literary antithesis, Candide, Zadig (cited by Sade), Justine and Juliette is not dissimilar. Sade is of course far more radical than Voltaire, in terms of both his narrative style and demands, and of the moral indictment that he does, in his own idiosyncratic fashion, formulate.

Hence Marcuse's statement that the problem of man's quest for liberty is given a more central place in the work of Sade than in that of any philosopher from Kant to Sartre. Artists such as Jean Cocteau perceived Sade in the same light, seeing him as a philosopher and, in his own way, a moralist.

Sade professes to have written "Justine ou les Infortunes de la Vertu" (1787) in just fifteen days. The eponymous heroine is, almost by definition, an exemplary figure. Plunged into penury at fourteen, she is doomed endlessly to flee those whose evil designs imperil her quest to keep her virtue and honour intact amid the turmoil of the 18th century. In an age in which honour required that people organise duels for the most fatuous bagatelles, Justine is forced to save her own – after a fashion. In a woman, honour was, of course, indistinguishable from sexual purity. This is the premise on which Sade constructs his paradox; though Justine is soon bereft of her virginity, her virtue is not on that account lost, since she insists that she has always resisted all attempts on it. And it is precisely her passivity amid torture and rape that preserves her virtue. She thus becomes a passive and passionless victim from whom all possibility of choice is torn; this, Sade seems to be telling us, is the fate of pure virtue. Moreover, the role played by predestination in the narrative suggests analogies with Christian doctrine. Her very "salvation" at Juliette's hands is not something that she has chosen; she is as passive in death as in life.

When, in 1979, Guido Crepax began adapting Sade's most popular work, "Justine", he was already a well known graphic artist. His popularity was primarily owed to his own original work, though he was, even then, making increasing use of classic models. Born 15 July 1933 in Milan, Guido Crepax's artistic talents came to the fore as early as his third year, when he began cutting out figures in newspaper without any preliminary sketches. Toys were hard to come by during the second world war, and Crepax invented his own, with their concomitant figures, rules and strategies. He also began reading comics like "Flash Gordon", "Mandrake and Phantom". His own first endeavours in the genre date from 1945, and include a cartoon version of James Whales' film "The Invisible Man": "I saw the film again many years later on television, looked out the album and leafed through it. It wasn't very well drawn, but it did give some notion of my narrative rhythms."

In 1947, however, Guido Crepax gave

Self-portrait by
Guido Crepax

up cartoons. During his architectural training, which he completed in 1958, he was forced to supplement his income, and began working in advertising as a graphic artist. There, paradoxically, he discovered his vocation. In 1957, he devised a publicity campaign for the petrol company Shell and won the Golden Palm of the advertising industry. Subsequently, Crepax worked for a number of agencies and magazines; in particular he drew some 200 cover pages for the medical journal "Tempo medico". "After a few childhood attempts, I did no more cartoons for a matter of years. I had forgotten all about them. I was working in graphics and advertising, mostly on album covers. In classical music, I illustrated the Beethoven symphonies, and I also did various things in jazz, which I really like. My real work with comic strips began much later, in 1965." In May 1965, the Italian comic-strip magazine "Linus" published the first episode of a Guido Crepax story; the main character was intended to be a superhero called Neutron, who in everyday life was the art critic Philip Rembrandt. The true heroine did not appear until the third episode. Her name was Valentina, and she was a reincarnation of the American actress Louise Brookes, who is best known for her performance in G.W. Pabst's 1929 film "Pandora's Box", based on Frank Wedekind's play "Die Büchse der Pandora" (1904). Valentina already showed a strong kinship with Justine, as she herself is made to say: "The Marquis de Sade says that Justine has the most beautiful buttocks in the world. Would he not say the same of mine?" Wolinski, another famous exponent of the genre, adds "Crepax draws the most beautiful buttocks in the history of the comic book. Take it from me. When it comes to comics, I know what I'm talking about." But Crepax has never simply been an erotic artist, and it would be wrong to define him merely as a creator of adult comic strips. It would be more accurate to say that under his pen, comic strips became adult. He made it possible to transpose into the world of the adult imagination the child's capacity to imagine fantastical possibilities and relationships. "I've drawn a total of sixty pages of Kafka's 'The Trial', which I think is one of the great books of the century. I also thought of doing 'The Magic Mountain' by Thomas Mann. The fact is, that I don't really like comic strips!" Crepax adds,

Publicity drawing for the oil company Shell

9

coquettishly. "So why do I draw them? Well, they seem to suit me ..." His wife Luisa explains: "You could say that traditional cartoon strips had become too narrow for Guido, and so he had to change them. He completely revolutionized the genre." He now undertook a variety of literary adaptations, including Robert Louis Stevenson's "Dr Jekyll and Mr Hyde" (1986), the stories of Edgar Allan Poe, Bram Stoker's "Dracula" (1983), and Henry James's "Turn of the Screw". Taking his inspiration from Jonathan Swift's masterpiece, "Gulliver's Travels", in 1983 Crepax published "I Viaggi di Bianca". Among his Valentina books, the most celebrated is "Lanterna magica" (1978). In this volume, Crepax completely eliminated text, creating a world of imagery whose many levels offered a multiplicity of interpretations. It can be thought of as a collection of isolated episodes or a complete story. We should also mention "A proposito di Valentina" (1975), which was not a cartoon book but a collection of drawings. The volume was dedicated to Louise Brooks, who wrote: "Besides Mr Pabst, you are the only person who has understood me – both without even meeting me except in films" (Letter from Louise Brooks to Guido Crepax, 3 May 1976).

Most of the books adapted by Crepax have also been filmed, but in his adaptations, Crepax has relied exclusively on the original texts. "I've never seen the film 'Histoire d'O'. When I illustrated 'Dracula', I was determined to be faithful to Bram Stoker. All the Dracula films distort the original work. Coppola's is the best. It appeared after I had drawn my own version in 1983. I said at the time "It's as if he'd read my version of 'Dracula'." Among the other Dracula films, the one I liked best was Murnau's 'Nosferatu', but he too departed considerably from the original. In the comic strip, what I like best is the 'montage' of images rather than simply telling a story." This poetic notion of the cartoon strip is best illustrated in the final images of his "Valentina pirata" volume. Valentina notes that in all narratives, only love and death count, and there is nothing new under the sun: "Anzi! Morte e amore! Non c'è niente di nuovo insomma ..." Her observation is taken up by her partner Rembrandt, who remarks "But in adventure stories, there is never anything really new! It's always a question of form, wouldn't you say?" ("Ma nelle avventure non c'è mai niente di veramente nuovo! È sempre una questione di forma, no?")

Louise Brooks, the model for Crepax's most famous character, Valentina

Fidelity to the text aptly describes Crepax's adaptation of "Justine". Of the three versions of the book, he chose the first, which was written in 1787 and first published in 1930; the other two

appeared in 1791 and 1797 respectively. Crepax finds an equivalent for the refined and somewhat abstract language of Sade – much of the power of whose narrative derives from his "obiter dicta" – in a subtle blend of distancing objectivity and dramatic choreography; this holds true of character and event alike. By way of introduction, Crepax show the Marquis as a faceless prisoner, quill in hand, writing, like Crepax himself, scenarios in which the imagination has full rein, in which the distinction between dream and reality is drastically attenuated. Sade wrote several of his works while confined to his prison cell; Crepax – no traveller he – wrote his scenarios in the seclusion of his apartment. It is striking that Crepax quotes the Marquis word for word, limiting himself to minor excisions; like the merest illustrator, he puts fidelity to the text before the image. The facelessness of both author and artist thus attenuates the distinction between Crepax and Sade. Indeed, the linearity of Crepax's opening pages presents an optical analogy with the lines of Sade's text. (Sade's works were, incidentally, illustrated by his contemporaries, so that Crepax's illustrations take their place in a living tradition.) Certain images do, nonetheless, allow of a distinction between the two highly individual creators. These are wordless frames, where the voice of the Marquis is silent, and the images are born exclusively of Crepax's narrative imagination. For the most part, they have a page to themselves and are therefore set apart from the narrative. In the brief respites accorded by Sade's imagination, the artist's inspiration takes flight, while the reader gains a well-earned repose. Crepax explains that he added these panels simply for the pleasure of drawing, after first sketching out the entire story. They had a secondary function, that of "conveying the atmosphere in which the events take place". Crepax frequently offers the reader a bird's-eye perspective, thus forcing him to distance himself in both space and time; the leading characters become the merest tesserae in a mosaic, and the reader seeks them as in a puzzle.

When Justine is depicted from above, sweeping, we see the unspoken burden of daily chores; when, after a series of tortures, she kneels in a little copse, the overhead perspective suggests the nameless, voiceless solitude of her presence amid an environment neither hostile nor sympathetic, but indifferent. It is by dint of such stylistic devices that Crepax takes his distance from Sade's narrative, placing himself and the reader at a remove from the locus of suffering. These nuances, and the atmosphere that they conjure, are attributable to Crepax alone, and transcend the bare bones of Sade's writing.

A part of the fascination of the story for the architect and artist in Crepax is the polarity between the two sisters, Juliette and Justine. This creates a geometrical narration whose self-abolition is its logical conclusion. When asked which of the two heroines he feels closest to, Crepax replies "I wanted to show that, in my view, Sade takes Justine's part, and not that of Juliette; Juliette is the very model of the 'sadist'." Crepax depicts Justine as a victim, but leaves no doubt that she is the true heroine. "It's a touching story, one is moved to tears at the end. Juliette too is saved by Justine – and therefore by Sade – since she tries to help Justine, and takes the veil after Justine's death." Before that fatal denouement, the two sisters embrace; union is restored. Justine saves not herself, but, in accordance with Christian tradition, someone else: her sister Juliette. She suffers that Juliette may be found and saved. Justine's death drives Juliette to enter a convent, thus restoring her to the bosom of the church. Sade's Justine is on the index of many countries, but is it in fact a new take on the conventional "life of the saint"? Juliette does not shrink from the sight of her dead sister, whose face is horribly deformed by a lightning strike. This frightening imago has an edifying effect like that of Christian images of saints; Justine thus becomes a singular development of the 'legenda aurea' of Christian martyrdom. Justine's trajectory can be read as a hagiography: like a saint who lives in a corrupt and immoral world, she attempts to preserve her virtue and is tortured for her convictions. Justine dies thunderstruck; thunder is one of the mythological attributes of the supreme deity; her death may therefore be seen as a direct translation to heaven.

The faceless writer (or artist?) in "Justine"

12

A prominent feature of Crepax's style in "Justine" and "Histoire d'O" is the slender elongated form of the bodies, not unlike those drawn by Aubrey Beardsley. This is combined with the scrupulous attention to detail that is one of Crepax's titles to mastery; ornament provides a running commentary on the story, while the choice of different sizes of image determines the pace and rhythm of the narrative. Unlike Sade, the teller of tales, Crepax the illustrator cannot help but endow his protagonists, those "missionaries of vice", with character. Names, synonyms and protagonists have to be supplied with a face and a body before they can join the dance. Even in their worst moments, Crepax's women retain a vestigial humanity, but the

Bird's-eye view from "Justine"

men resemble wild beasts. The grimacing faces of men such as 'Père' Antonin are grotesque as the gargoyles of Notre-Dame. By contrast, the serenity and reach of Crepax's landscapes are reminiscent of Japanese prints, in which the figures are lost like structuralist metaphors. The frequent use made by Crepax in "Justine" and "Histoire d'O" of subtle variations in the shade of grey forms a marked contrast with his earlier works, from which they are almost completely absent.

"In my view – this is my own interpretation – Sade was not an apologist for Sadism; he was much more concerned with psychological violence. 'The Misfortunes of Virtue' in 'Justine' are not simply tales of suffering; they are not, in essence, physical. In my view, Sadism is not – at least in the works of Sade – a matter of violence. Sade is not responsible for the 'Sadism' we see in reality. We know that those who tortured human beings in the camps took pleasure in what they did. They were 'Sadists', but that's not Sade's fault. Yet, because of the derivation of the word, he has been given a share of blame for things which are nothing to do with him."

Crepax gives particular emphasis to Sade's critique of Catholic dogma, singling out for attention the words of the thieving Mme Dubois. If God existed, Evil would not prevail on earth; since it does, either God wills it so, or He is too weak to prevent it. Either way, the Marquis concludes, fear of God is superfluous.

A outline summary of the story of Justine is of little service, since it does no justice to

Sade's reflections on the events he describes. These return again and again to the polarity of "Good" and "Evil"; these two rather academic extremes are given a very un-academic and radical treatment. Good is punished, Evil is rewarded. Sade takes great pleasure in analysing traditional values; he first inverts them, then challenges the reader to protest or concur. The world appears to confirm his theses, while nonetheless awaiting a "Yes, but". "Nature created us all equal", declares Mme Dubois to Justine. "If fate takes pleasure in disrupting this first state ..., it is for us to correct her whims, and remedy the usurpations of 'force majeure' by our own ingenuity."

In Crepax's stories, references to the characters and works of Sade began well before his adaptation of Justine. Thus the dreams of "Valentina" show sadistic and masochistic tendencies. In addition to these generalised influences, we find direct quotations in the form of literary reference. Another of Crepax's heroines, "Bianca", first appeared in 1969, six years before his "Justine"; on the bookshelves in her bedroom we see a copy of Sade's "Juliette". In "Bianca", the name Juliette is borne by Bianca's antagonist, who acts as the assistant of Mlle Squelette, a monitor in a girl's boarding-school.

Sadism has many faces (Père Antonin from "Justine")

The gulf between the often willfully misunderstood terms of sadism and masochism is already present in the figure of Crepax's most popular creation, Valentina, who was herself inspired by the character Lulu played by Louise Brooks in Pabst's film "Pandora's Box". One of the key scenes in this film is the murder of Lulu by Jack the Ripper (played by Gustav Diessl). With certain other episodes of the film, such as the death of Doctor Schön (played by Fritz Kortner) and the richly detailed music-hall scenes, it counts among the most beautiful scenes in the film and indeed of the entire era. The erotic fantasies of the young Valentina are haunted by the Freudian couple love and death, Eros and Thanatos, which find their equivalents in many of the stories that unfold in her imagination.

Crepax created his version of the "Histoire d'O" in three parts. The first was completed in 1973, the second in 1974 and the last in 1984/5. The first and second parts take place in the 20s, while the third is set in the 80s, the decade when Crepax was drawing it. Crepax adapts his style to the epoch. In the first two parts, the contrast of black and white is a major feature, while the line, décor and environment of the first two chapters is much influenced by Beardsley and Art Nouveau. In the third and fourth chapters, we recognize the familiar page-boy haircut of the 20s. The rationalist Bauhaus aesthetic and severe architecture make for a rather cold style of representation; a similar atmosphere can be found in the work of the Italian artist, Cagnaccio di San Pietro. The last part of "O", set some fifty years later, shows the powerful influence exerted by Italian "haute couture", notably in the emblems of power and the phallic symbols by which wealth is connoted in that society. The first and second parts are primarily concerned with the power relations of individuals; the third part associates the aspiration to power with capitalist values. Here it is no longer individual actions, nor the concomitant abuse of physical strength, that prevails; economic actions alone have the power to enslave.

Crepax's "Histoire d'O" reads, on the one hand, like a journey through an epoch decisive in the history of sexual liberation; on the other, by changing the setting and decors, Crepax encompasses the timeless aspect of O's story. In the first volume of "O", Crepax's narration is carried almost exclusively by images, and words are reduced to a bare minimum. The rhythm of the narrative is often interrupted by pages three-quarters blank; one, indeed, is completely black. The story exhibits in symptomatic fashion the geometry characteristic of Crepax's framing of images, which also serves to reflect the "geometry of relations". Thus, at one point O's face is found at the centre of a pentagon surrounded by a balletic array of sexual acts. The five outer images are asymmetrical, giving an impression both of spiral movement and of a spider's web, the latter through intermittent glimpses of a circular motif in the carpet. The sexual act itself is shown as faceless, but at its centre is a head and a face. For Crepax, eroticism lies in the head rather in sexual excess.

A poetics of intertextuality: the author of "Justine" figures in Bianca's bookshelves

On another page, the circular movement is replaced by radial sections. At the centre, the focus is on bodies, and the sexual act is again faceless, but it is surrounded by hands and faces. It is as if O and her female lover had become two Eves in a paradise whose geometry testifies to its artificiality.

"Histoire d'O" was published in 1954, by one Pauline Réage. Réage proved to be a pseudonym, and the true identity of the author was sought in the pantheon of male writers; names such as André Pieyre de Mandiargues, François Mauriac and Jean Paulhan were suggested. Only in 1995 did the identity of the author finally emerge. Her name is Dominique Aury, and she was Jean Paulhan's mistress, who collaborated with him in the publication of the works of Sade. "Histoire d'O" was a best-seller in which Sade and Sacher-Masoch seemed to combine; on Aury's own account, she wished to create fantasies whose defining characteristic was not a "feminine" or "masculine" perspective, but simply that of sincerity. "Histoire d'O" was not Aury's only literary success; her "Anthologie de la poésie religieuse française" was also much admired. Here, then, the circle that began with the hagiographic structures of "Justine" may be said to close.

In 1975, two years after Crepax had begun to illustrate Aury's story, Just Jaeckin, who had earned worldwide fame with his 1973 film "Emmanuelle", adapted "Histoire d'O" for the cinema. The former model Corinne Clery made her debut in the central role, which had been unsuccessfully offered to Jacqueline Bisset, Sidne Rome and Charlotte Rampling. Another of Jaeckin's films was "Gwendoline", the story of a cartoon character created by John Willie and Eric Stanton, whose work was sometimes compared to that of Crepax. Crepax praised their work, but denied the analogy. "Histoire d'O II – Chapter II" was prepared by Julian Temple but was eventually made by its producer, Eric Rochat. Cinema experts such as Georg Seesslen perceive Julan Temple's influence only in the design of the film, and regret that the film never became "a cinematic equivalent of the erotic cartoon strip fantasy".

Before drawing "Histoire d'O" in 1973, Crepax produced one of his most unusual works, the adventures of a man named U. The story was devised in 1970-71 and published for the first time in April 1975, in "Linus"; the preface by Emilo Tadini made reference to what was then Crepax's most famous adaptation of a work of erotic literature in its title: "Histoire d'U". U is an intellectual living in the none-too-distant future. With the exception of a few young rebels who are soon dispatched, he is the only human being on planet earth, which is now inhabited by anthropomorphic animals. The question remains, whether they are truly animals, or whether this is simply a delusion of U's.

It has often been said that the heroines of "Histoire d'O" are less women than objects of desire. But here too the question arises whether they are true human beings or mere projections. In this respect, O's story is not dissimilar to that of U. While he was working on the first episodes of "Histoire d'O", Crepax introduced a similar theme into one of Valentina's adventures. In a sort of jump-cut, without any preparation, Valentina suddenly finds herself in the 30s, and wonders why: "I suspect that there is an ... O ...?" Suddenly she discovers on her buttocks the brand born by O, and protests at the trappings and story imposed on her. This self-quotation shows Crepax as a sort of ringmaster or MC, happily playing one story off against another, while seeking to maintain an ironic distance. As a parting remark, is there no resemblance between the circular sign that Crepax uses to sign his work and an 'O'? And are not all of Crepax's works therefore "Stories of an 'O'"?

The eye as erotic organ (from "Lanterna magica")

Roland Barthes, in his interpretation of the work, took the view that O's erotic organ was the ear. In Crepax, by contrast, the erotic organ is always the eye. It is at once more eloquent and more truthful than the mouth. Words are codes; the eye decodes. This explains the face- and animal-masks of "Histoire d'O", behind which language is concealed or abolished. Whereas in "Justine" it is the framing text that conducts the reader, in "O" it is the wordless image-fragments that preside; in these, faceless bodies or parts of bodies seemingly without context ensure the progress of the action, in a manner purely mechanical and often entirely artificial. Closed eyes symbolize the option of silence in the refusal of the erotic. With every eye that opens, the quest for the erotic recommences.

Justine

Prologue

PHILOSOPHY'S GREATEST TRIUMPH WOULD BE TO SHED LIGHT ON THE DARK PATHS TRACED BY PROVIDENCE TO REACH ITS ENDS CONCERNING MAN, AND MOREOVER TO DRAW ON THAT BASIS A LAW OF CONDUCT THAT MIGHT GUIDE THIS UNHAPPY CREATURE IN INTERPRETING THE WILL OF SUCH PROVIDENCE AND CHOOSING THE RIGHT PATH TO AVOID THE BIZARRE WHIMS OF FATE, WHICH IS GIVEN A THOUSAND NAMES WITHOUT EVER BEING DEFINED...

... BECAUSE IF ACTING IN ACCORDANCE WITH SOCIAL NORMS AND NEVER ABANDONING THE RESPECT WE HAVE BEEN TAUGHT TO FEEL TOWARD THEM, WE SHOULD HAPPEN, THROUGH THE EVIL OF OTHERS, TO BE PIERCED BY A THOUSAND THORNS WHILE THE WICKED FIND ONLY ROSES, WILL NOT THE PEOPLE WHO LACK A FOUNDATION OF VIRTUE SOLID ENOUGH TO TRANSCEND THE QUESTIONS AROUSED BY SUCH CIRCUMSTANCES RESOLVED THAT IT IS BETTER TO FLOW WITH THE RIVER'S CURRENTS RATHER THAN FIGHT AGAINST IT?

WILL THEY NOT DECLARE THAT VIRTUE, BEAUTIFUL AS IT MAY BE, IS SOMETIMES SADLY TOO WEAK TO STRUGGLE AGAINST VICE, AND THEREFORE BECOMES THE LOSING SIDE IN A CENTURY SO RADICALLY CORRUPT THAT THE SAFEST THING TO DO IS TO JOIN THE EVILDOERS?

THESE ARE THE FEELINGS THAT BROUGHT US...

... TO PICK UP THE PEN AND IN GOOD FAITH...

... REQUEST THE READER'S ATTENTION AND INTEREST...

...TOWARD THE MISFORTUNES OF THE SAD AND MISERABLE **JUSTINE**...

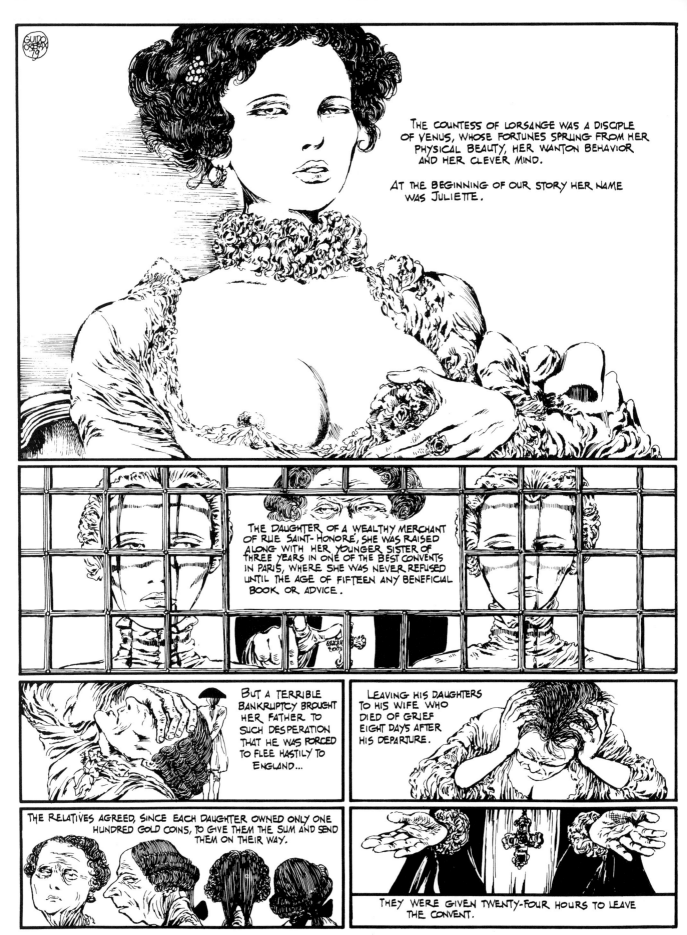

THE COUNTESS OF LORSANGE WAS A DISCIPLE OF VENUS, WHOSE FORTUNES SPRUNG FROM HER PHYSICAL BEAUTY, HER WANTON BEHAVIOR AND HER CLEVER MIND.

AT THE BEGINNING OF OUR STORY HER NAME WAS JULIETTE.

THE DAUGHTER OF A WEALTHY MERCHANT OF RUE SAINT-HONORÉ, SHE WAS RAISED ALONG WITH HER YOUNGER SISTER OF THREE YEARS IN ONE OF THE BEST CONVENTS IN PARIS, WHERE SHE WAS NEVER REFUSED UNTIL THE AGE OF FIFTEEN ANY BENEFICIAL BOOK OR ADVICE.

BUT A TERRIBLE BANKRUPTCY BROUGHT HER FATHER TO SUCH DESPERATION THAT HE WAS FORCED TO FLEE HASTILY TO ENGLAND...

LEAVING HIS DAUGHTERS TO HIS WIFE WHO DIED OF GRIEF EIGHT DAYS AFTER HIS DEPARTURE.

THE RELATIVES AGREED, SINCE EACH DAUGHTER OWNED ONLY ONE HUNDRED GOLD COINS, TO GIVE THEM THE SUM AND SEND THEM ON THEIR WAY.

THEY WERE GIVEN TWENTY-FOUR HOURS TO LEAVE THE CONVENT.

24

25

LET US LEAVE JUSTINE FOR A MOMENT, AND RETURN TO JULIETTE TO LET YOU KNOW HOW, IN FIFTEEN YEARS, SHE BECAME A NOBLEWOMAN, WITH AN INCOME OF 30,000 POUNDS, FINE JEWELRY, TWO OR THREE HOMES IN PARIS AS WELL AS THE COUNTRY AND, AT THE MOMENT, THE LOVE, WEALTH AND TRUST OF MONSIEUR DE CORVILLE, COUNSELOR OF STATE...

THE ROAD, NO DOUBT, WAS FULL OF THORNS...

UPON LEAVING THE CONVENT JULIETTE WENT TO SEE A WOMAN SHE HAD HEARD ABOUT...

HOW OLD ARE YOU, CHILD?

FIFTEEN, IN A FEW DAYS!

AND NO ONE EVER...?

OH, NO MADAME I ASSURE YOU!

VERY WELL, LOVELY... YOU CAN STAY HERE... JUST ALWAYS FOLLOW MY ADVICE... SHOW KINDNESS TO THE GIRLS... AND CRAFTINESS TO MEN!

27

FROM THEN ON SHE WAS A DAUGHTER OF THE HOUSE... SHARING ALL THE DUTIES, SUBMITTING TO BIZARRE TASTES AND PERVERSE FANTASIES...

SHE WAS DRIVEN BY A DESIRE FOR PLEASURE AS WELL AS BY A SELF-DESTRUCTIVE STREAK WHICH DULLED THE IMAGINATION, ALLOWING IT TO BLOOM ONLY IN THE MIDST OF EXCESS.

THIS SECOND SCHOOL COMPLETED THE CORRUPTION OF JULIETTE'S MORES AND THE TRIUMPHS SHE SAW SPROUTING FROM VICE, UTTERLY DEGRADED HER SOUL...

SHE WAS FANCIED BY A DEPRAVED OLD GENTLEMAN WHO BEGAN TO SUPPORT HER AFTER INITIALLY REQUESTING HER SERVICES FOR ONLY FIFTEEN MINUTES...

SHE KNEW HOW TO EXPLOIT HIM AND BEGAN TO ATTEND THE THEATRE... STROLL PROMENADES ALONGSIDE PROMINENT MEMBERS OF SOCIETY... SHE WAS SEEN... SHE WAS MENTIONED... SHE WAS ENVIED...

WHEN JULIETTE WAS TWENTY, A CERTAIN COUNT OF LORSANGE BECAME SO TAKEN WITH HER THAT HE RESOLVED TO GIVE HER HIS NAME... AN INCOME OF TWELVE THOUSAND POUNDS... A HOUSE... SERVANTS... A STANDARD... AND HIS INHERITANCE IN CASE OF PREMATURE DEATH...

AT THIS POINT JULIETTE GAVE IN TO THE DARK DESIRE OF CUTTING SHORT HER HUSBAND'S DAYS...

ONCE AGAIN FREE, AND NOW A COUNTESS, THE LADY OF LORSANGE RESUMED HER OLD HABITS... SHE GAVE HERSELF FOR 200 GOLD LOUIS... 500 FOR A MONTH...

UNTIL THE AGE OF 26 SHE MADE NUMEROUS CONQUESTS, SHE RUINED THREE AMBASSADORS... FOUR MERCHANTS... TWO BISHOPS... THREE KNIGHTS OF THE KING'S ORDER...

As one crime often leads to another, the wretched Juliette stained herself with two more like the first... to these horrors she added two or three infanticides...

... These crimes were ignored like the others...

... and didn't keep this clever and ambitious woman from finding new victims every day, which rapidly increased her wealth.

Is it true then that wealth can be found in the company of crime and in the midst of the most deliberate corruption and chaos, the thread of existence can be gilded by that which we call luck?

Do not be alarmed by this cruel and fatal truth! May the example that we're about to offer, of bad luck plaguing virtue, not disturb the souls of honest people... The wealth found in crime is only an illusion... the guilty harbor within them a worm that eats at them relentlessly, and keeps them from enjoying the happiness that surrounds them, leaving only the memory of their crimes... while the unfortunate soul plagued with bad luck finds relief in his own conscience, and the secret joys found in the purity of soul are the reward for human injustice!

SUCH WAS THE STORY OF THE COUNTESS OF LORSANGE, WHEN MONSIEUR DE CORVILLE DECIDED TO SACRIFICE HIMSELF COMPLETELY FOR HER AND TIE HER IRREVOCABLY TO HIMSELF...

ARE YOU TIRED?

YES... SHALL WE STOP IN MONTARGIS?

ONE NIGHT IN JUNE THEY STAYED AT THE INN WHERE THE STAGECOACH TO LYON MADE A STOP...

WHERE ARE YOU TAKING HER? WHAT HAS SHE DONE?

SHE'S ACCUSED OF BURGLARY, MURDER AND ARSON... BUT I CONFESS I WAS NEVER MORE RELUCTANT TO MAKE AN ARREST.

SHE'S THE GENTLEST OF CREATURES AND WOULD SEEM THE MOST HONEST...

HM... COULDN'T THIS BE ONE OF THOSE MISTAKES SO COMMON IN PROVINCIAL COURTS? WHERE WAS THE CRIME COMMITTED?

NEAR LYON... SHE'S GOING TO PARIS TO CONFIRM THE SENTENCE AND WILL RETURN TO LYON TO BE EXECUTED!

PLEASE DARLING... HAVE HER RELEASED... AT LEAST FOR ONE NIGHT... YOU HAVE THE AUTHORITY! DO IT FOR ME...

I WOULD LIKE TO REQUEST CUSTODY OF THE PRISONER... I'M A COUNSELOR IN PARIS AND WILL BE PERSONALLY RESPONSIBLE.

VERY WELL, SIR!

THIS MISERABLE CREATURE COULD BE INNOCENT, BUT IS TREATED AS A CRIMINAL... AND I LIVE IN LUXURY, WHILE I'M CERTAINLY MORE GUILTY THAN SHE IS.

TELL ME... WHAT HAPPENED?... I... I WOULD LIKE TO KNOW...

MADAME, THE STORY OF MY LIFE MIGHT SEEM PROOF THAT VIRTUE LEADS TO MISFORTUNE... IT MIGHT BE SEEN AS A COMPLAINT AGAINST PROVIDENCE... AND I AM ASHAMED...

... ALLOW ME TO CONCEAL MY NAME... MY BIRTH WAS NOT NOBLE, BUT HONEST AND I WAS NOT DESTINED TO THE HUMILIATION FROM WHICH MOST OF MY ILLS WERE BORN...

Dubourg, Du Harpin, Dubois, St. Florent

...I WON'T MENTION MY FIRST DISMAL EXPERIENCES... WHEN I RAN OUT OF MONEY I LOOKED FOR WORK WITH A WEALTHY PARISIAN BUSINESS MAN NAMED DUBOURG...

AFTER WAITING TWO HOURS IN HIS FOYER...

THIS WAS ABOUT THIRTEEN YEARS AGO...

COME ON IN!... MONSIEUR HAS AWOKEN AND WILL RECEIVE YOU NOW...

THAT'S ENOUGH!... YOU CAN GO NOW... WELL, MY DEAR, WHAT DO YOU WANT?

...I'M HERE BECAUSE... YOU MUST KNOW, I'M ALONE IN THE WORLD...

COME HERE, TELL ME EVERYTHING...

...I SEE... TELL ME THEN... ARE YOU STILL AN HONEST GIRL?

OH, MONSIEUR... IF I WERE NOT I WOULDN'T BE SO POOR... OR SO EMBARASSED...

IF MY WEALTH IS TO SUPPORT YOU, WHAT CAN YOU OFFER IN RETURN?

TO SERVE MONSIEUR...

THAT'S ALL I ASK...

THE SERVICES OF A CHILD LIKE YOU ARE NOT VERY USEFUL! YOU HAVE NEITHER THE AGE NOR THE BUILD... BUT WITH MORE OF AN OPEN MIND YOU MIGHT FIND YOUR FORTUNE BY GIVING PLEASURE TO LIBERTINES... YOU UNDERSTAND?

36

38

40

41

IT'S TRUE... THERE ISN'T MUCH WORK!...

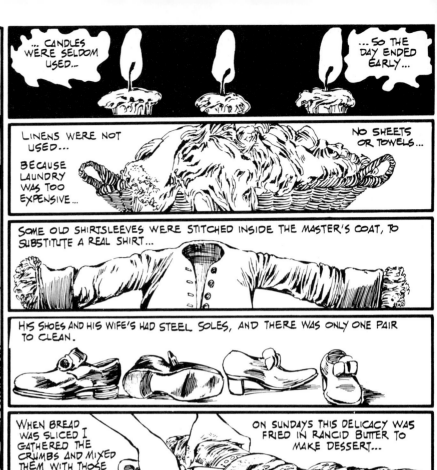

... CANDLES WERE SELDOM USED...

...SO THE DAY ENDED EARLY...

LINENS WERE NOT USED...

BECAUSE LAUNDRY WAS TOO EXPENSIVE...

NO SHEETS OR TOWELS...

SOME OLD SHIRTSLEEVES WERE STITCHED INSIDE THE MASTER'S COAT, TO SUBSTITUTE A REAL SHIRT...

HIS SHOES AND HIS WIFE'S HAD STEEL SOLES, AND THERE WAS ONLY ONE PAIR TO CLEAN.

WHEN BREAD WAS SLICED I GATHERED THE CRUMBS AND MIXED THEM WITH THOSE LEFT AFTER DINNER...

ON SUNDAYS THIS DELICACY WAS FRIED IN RANCID BUTTER TO MAKE DESSERT...

IN A TINY ROOM WITHOUT WALLPAPER, THE PLASTER WAS SCRAPED WITH A KNIFE TO GET POWDER FOR MY MASTER'S WIG AND MADAME'S PONYTAIL...

44

46

48

50

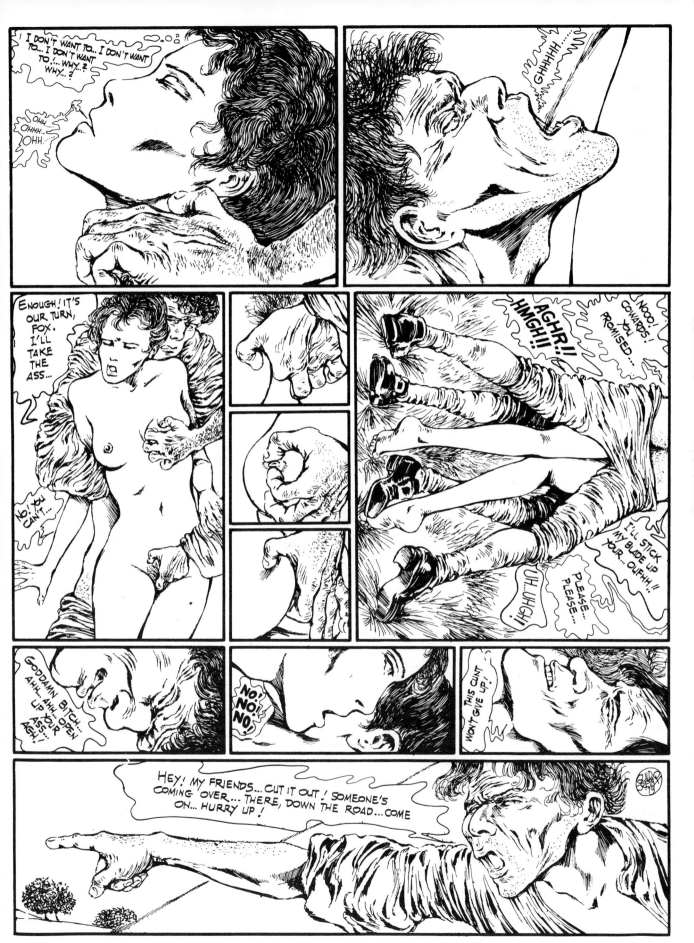

51

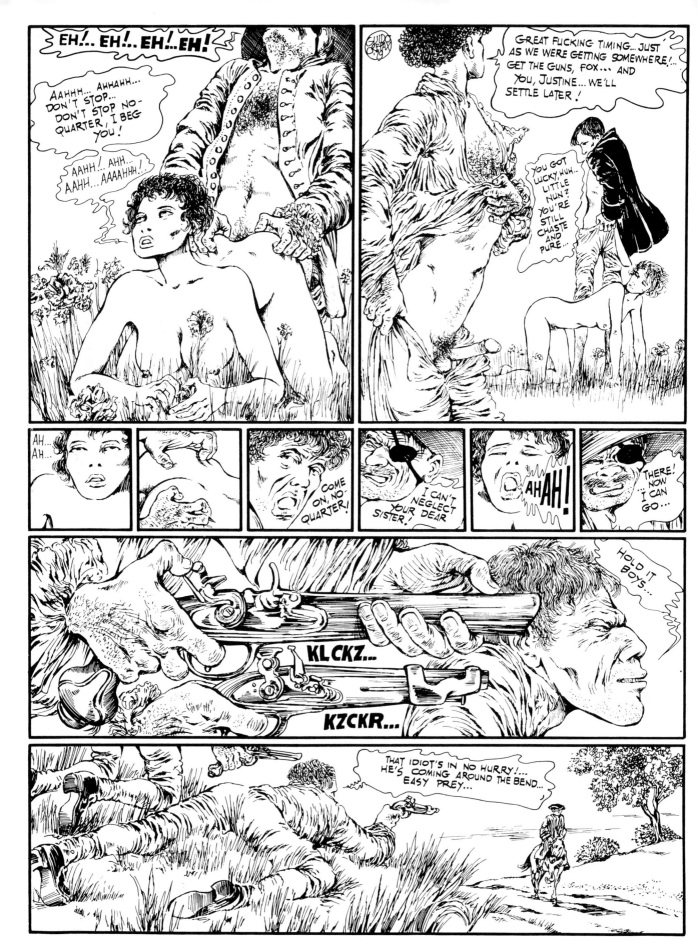

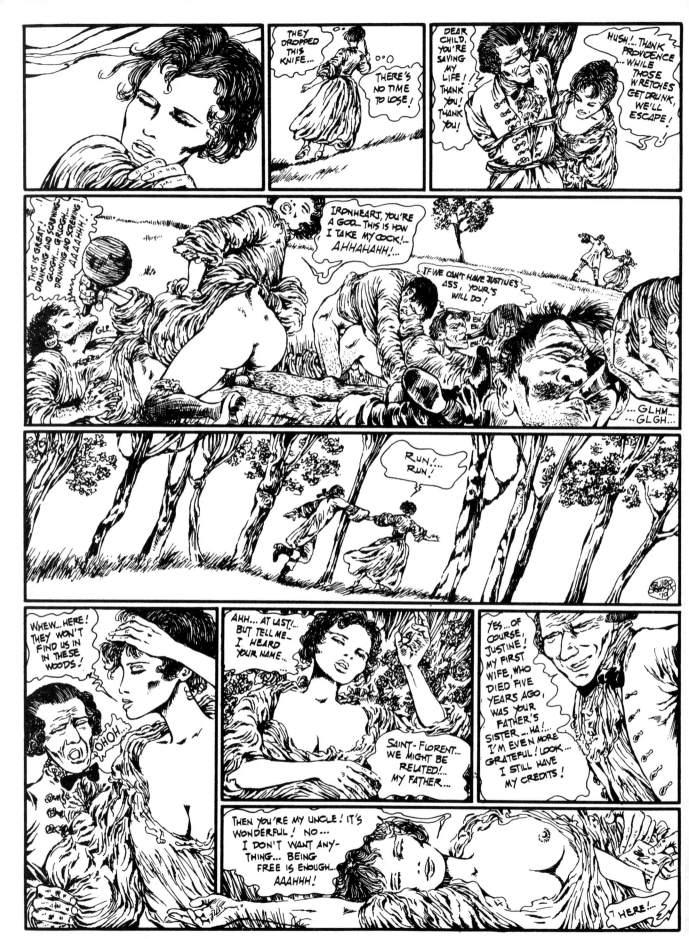

59

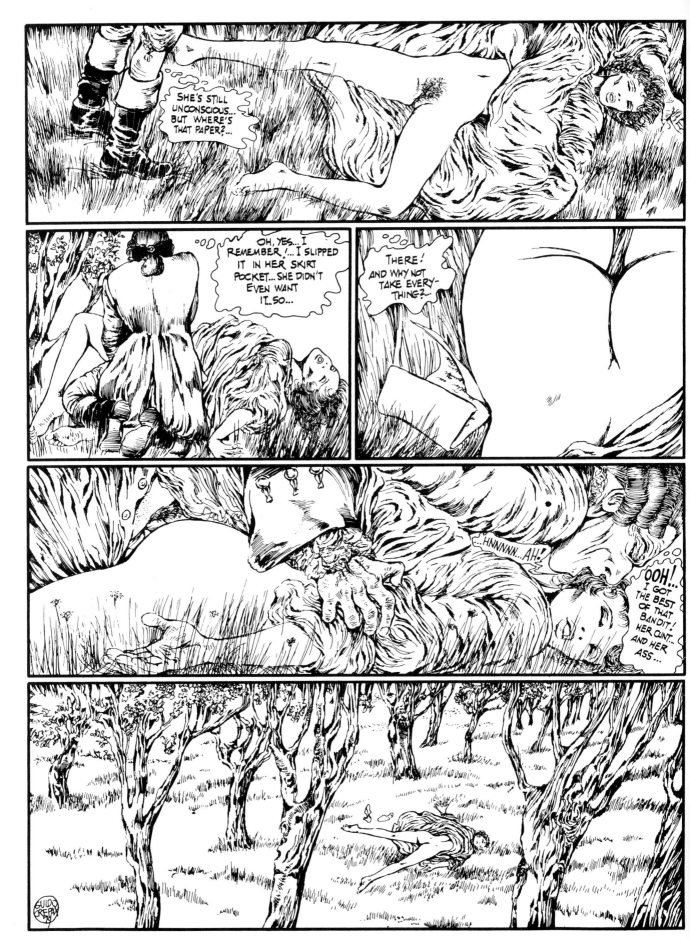

The Marquis
du Bressac

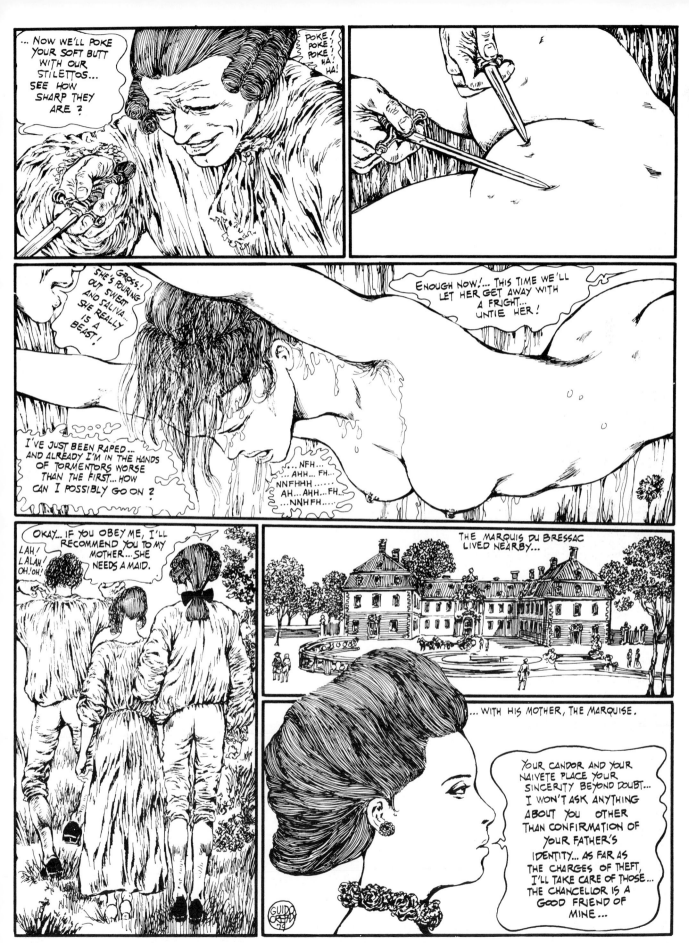

67

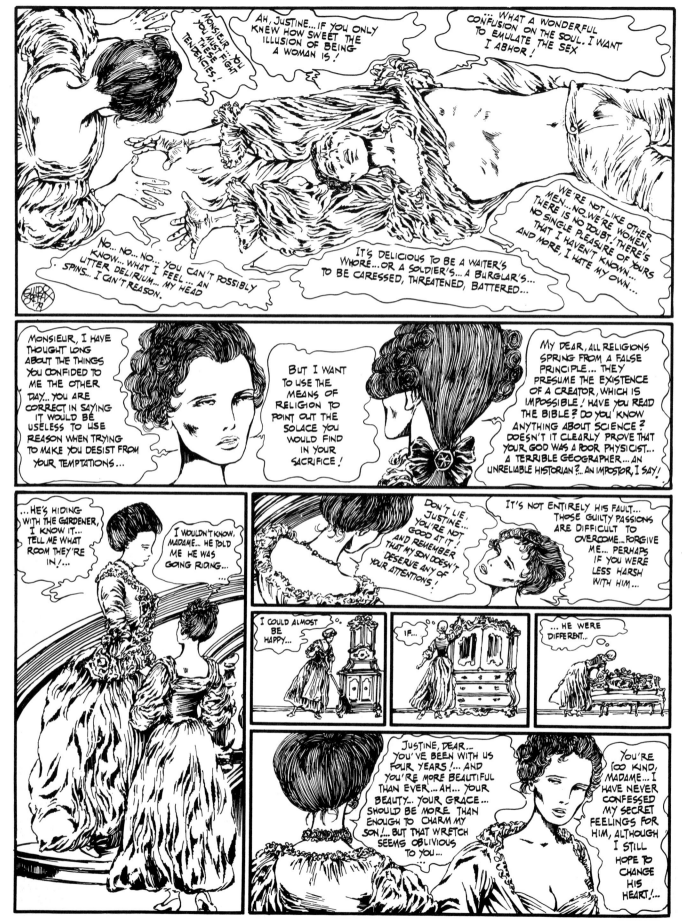

70

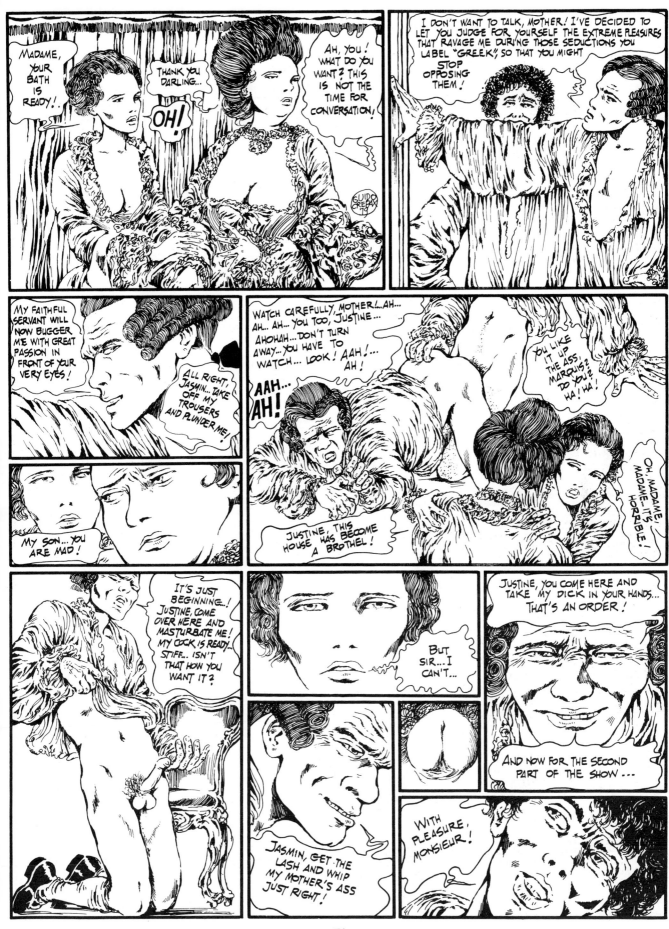

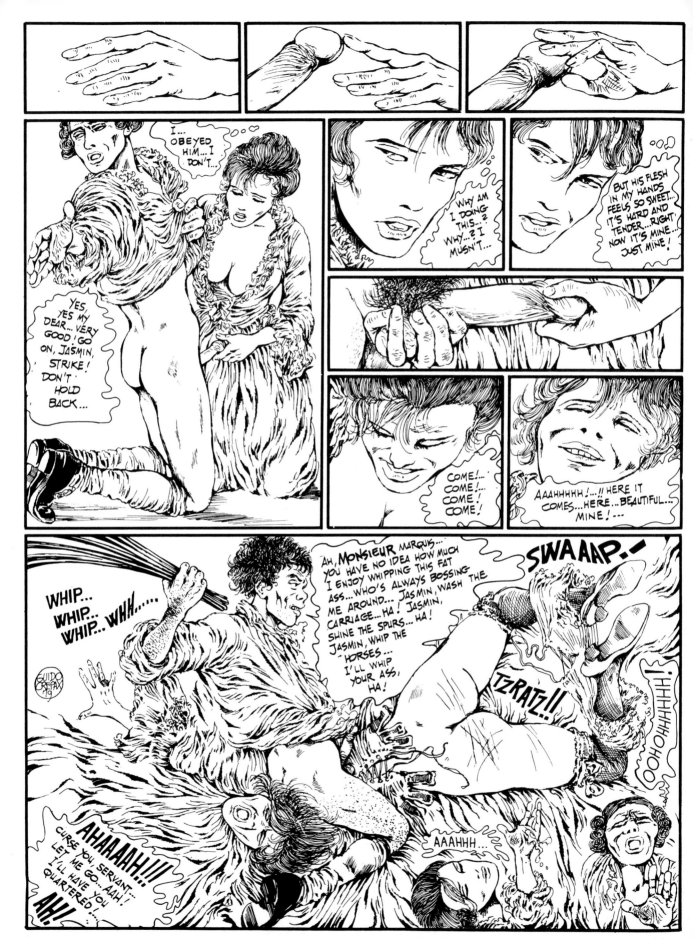

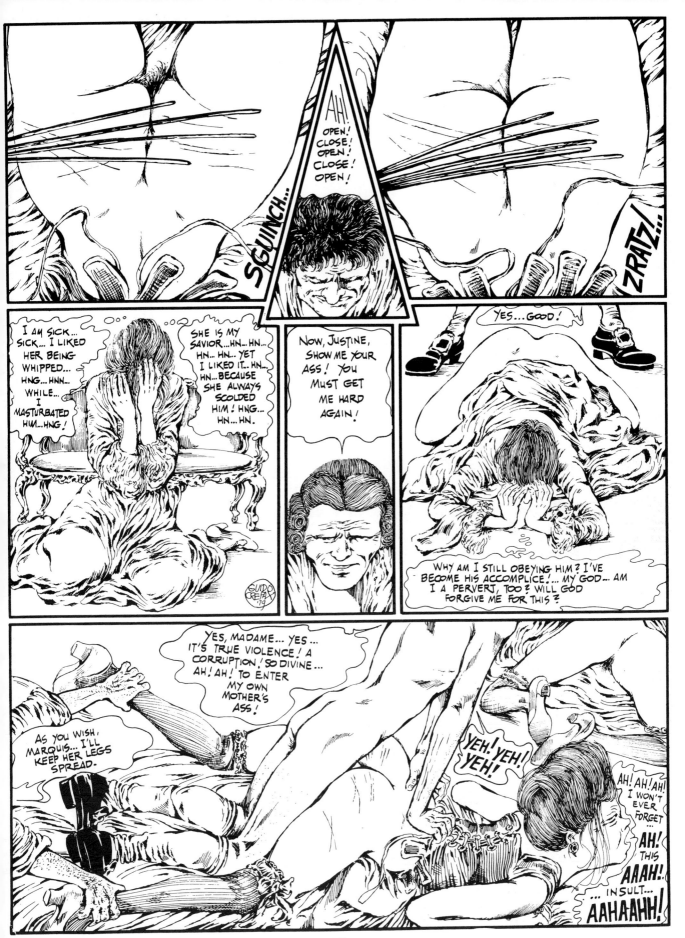

MADAME!... MADAME!... THEY'VE LEFT... OH, GOD! SHE'S UNCONSCIOUS... HOW CAN I CONSOLE HER? I DIDN'T EVEN TRY TO HELP HER... IS IT RIGHT OF ME TO PASSIVELY SUBMIT TO VIOLENCE, WITHOUT A FIGHT? AND WORSE... I'M IN LOVE WITH THE MAN RESPONSIBLE FOR THIS!

AHHHH...

FOR DAYS I'VE BEEN WONDERING WHY I STILL STAY HERE, IN THIS HOUSE OF TURPITUDES...

...I WOULDN'T KNOW WHERE TO GO... THAT'S WHY I STAY HERE... I KNOW IT...AND HAVE NO PEACE BECAUSE OF IT.

JUSTINE!

AH... MONSIEUR!

YOUR ORDERS?

LISTEN... THE TIME HAS COME FOR YOU TO SHOW ME ULTIMATE PROOF OF YOUR LOYALTY!

YOU KNOW I WOULD NEVER BETRAY YOUR TRUST...

...ANYWAY, YOU KNOW THE RISK YOU'D BE RUNNING IF YOU BETRAYED ME.

THE WORST PUNISHMENT WOULD BE IF YOU LOST YOUR FAITH IN ME! I DON'T NEED OTHER THREATS...

TELL ME...

VERY WELL... I WANT MY MOTHER KILLED... AND YOU WILL BE THE ONE TO EXECUTE HER!

ME?! NO, MONSIEUR... DON'T ASK FOR THAT!...

JUSTINE... YOUR NAIVE EYES ARE FACING TWO CRIMES...THE KILLING OF A HUMAN BEING, AND THE AGGRAVATION THAT THE VICTIM IS MY OWN MOTHER... BUT MAN DOES NOT HAVE THE POWER TO DESTROY!... AT THE MOST HE HAS THE POWER TO ALTER FORMS...

EVERY SUBSTANCE IS THE SAME IN FRONT OF NATURE! WHAT DOES IT MATTER IF THE MASS OF FLESH THAT TODAY IS A WOMAN, IS TOMORROW TURNED INTO THE SUBSTANCE OF A THOUSAND DIFFERENT WORMS AND INSECTS.

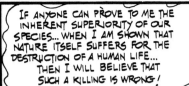

IF ANYONE CAN PROVE TO ME THE INHERENT SUPERIORITY OF OUR SPECIES... WHEN I AM SHOWN THAT NATURE ITSELF SUFFERS FOR THE DESTRUCTION OF A HUMAN LIFE... THEN I WILL BELIEVE THAT SUCH A KILLING IS WRONG!

HOW COULD I EVER HAVE FELT LOVE FOR THIS INSANE, AMORAL DEGENERATE?...

I'LL PRETEND TO AGREE TO HIS MONSTROSITIES, AND THEN TRY TO SAVE MADAME!...

AS FAR AS MATRICIDE... I FIND IT INSIGNIFICANT!

...BUT ONLY THEIR FATHER'S!

TAKING INTO ACCOUNT THAT INFANTS ARE FORMED, NOT BY THEIR MOTHER'S BLOOD...

THE WOMAN BREAST CONSERVES AND ELABORATES BUT GIVES NOTHING ITS OWN!

I OWE YOU MY ALLEGIANCE!

HA! I KNEW I WOULD WIN OVER YOUR RELUCTANCE... YOU'LL ACT FOR MY LOVE!

YOU'LL SEE... IT'LL BE EASY... JUST MIX POISON IN WITH MY MOTHER'S MORNING TEA.

YOU'RE THE FIRST WOMAN I'VE EVER KISSED! I'LL REWARD YOU WITH TWO THOUSAND GOLD PIECES EVERY YEAR...

... I'VE LONGED FOR THIS SO MUCH... AND NOW I FEEL SO COLD ABOUT THIS MAN...

DRLNG! DRLNG!

I'M SET TO INHERIT SIXTY-THOUSAND POUNDS... WE MUST CELEBRATE!

DID YOU CALL, SIR?

HOW CAN I HELP?

MISERABLE... DESPICABLE MAN... I WOULD HAVE ACCEPTED EVERYTHING... EVEN HIS VICES... BUT HE'S ONLY A VULGAR THIEF AND MURDERER... HE DOESN'T EVEN HAVE THAT SORT OF GREATNESS THAT GOES WITH THE DEMON OF PERVERSITY!... AND HE'S STUPID ENOUGH TO THINK HE CAN CORRUPT ME...

YOUR ASS, MY BOY! JUSTINE HAS THE MOST BEAUTIFUL ASS, BUT IT'S NOT FOR ME... GO ON JUSTINE, UNDRESS HIM AND CARESS MY COCK!

PLEASE BE MORE GENTLE THAN JASMIN!

IS THIS ALL RIGHT, SIR?

I'LL FUCK THIS YOUNG GYPSY IN YOUR HONOR, MY DEAR!

JUSTINE... JUSTINE! IT'S TRUE THAT LUCK COMES WITH CRIME! ONLY TWO DAYS AGO, I PLANNED MY MOTHER'S DEATH, AND NOW I HAVE RECEIVED NEWS OF A LARGE INHERITANCE FROM A FORGOTTEN UNCLE!

IT IS TRULY GOOD NEWS IF IT WILL CONVINCE YOU TO ABANDON YOUR PLAN!

NOT AT ALL! THIS PROVES BEYOND A DOUBT THAT THE MERE IDEA OF A CRIME ATTRACTS GOOD LUCK! OBVIOUSLY IT FAVORS VILLAINY...

THERE'S NO TIME TO LOSE... I MUST WARN MADAME!

BESIDES HIS HORRIBLE CYNICISM, HE HAS THAT SUPERSTITION... THAT PROVIDENCE STRIKES AGAINST THE WEAK INSTEAD OF PROTECTING THEM...WHAT IF...?

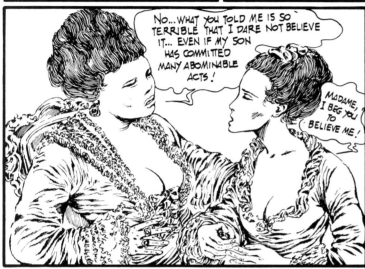

NO...WHAT YOU TOLD ME IS SO TERRIBLE THAT I DARE NOT BELIEVE IT... EVEN IF MY SON HAS COMMITTED MANY ABOMINABLE ACTS!

MADAME, I BEG YOU TO BELIEVE ME!

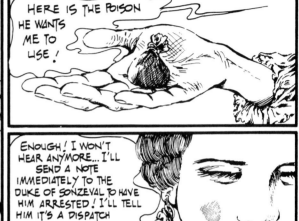

HERE IS THE POISON HE WANTS ME TO USE!

ENOUGH! I WON'T HEAR ANYMORE... I'LL SEND A NOTE IMMEDIATELY TO THE DUKE OF SONZEVAL TO HAVE HIM ARRESTED! I'LL TELL HIM IT'S A DISPATCH CONCERNING HIS NEW INHERITANCE...

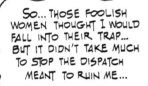

SO... THOSE FOOLISH WOMEN THOUGHT I WOULD FALL INTO THEIR TRAP... BUT IT DIDN'T TAKE MUCH TO STOP THE DISPATCH MEANT TO RUIN ME...

MY MOTHER DOESN'T REALIZE THAT THE SERVANTS ARE MORE LOYAL TO ME THAN HER... SHE GAVE HERSELF AWAY WITH A GLANCE... NOW MY REVENGE WILL BE TERRIBLE!

HOLD THEM BACK, JASMIN... THEY'RE HUNGRY, HUH? SOON THEY'LL BE SATISFIED... AS WILL YOU, MY DEAR JOSEPH...COME ALONG!

EH! EH! EH!

...AHRGH... AHRH... AHRH... GRRRRRRR.... GRRRR...

GRROHH... OHRH...

GHRAH... AHRGH!

GOR... GOR...

Doctor Rodin

I'VE A NEW HOME AND YET I STILL DON'T KNOW WHAT'S IN STORE FOR ME... I'VE NO EXPECTATIONS, BUT I'M GOING TO WRITE TO THE MARQUIS...

... HE SHOULD AT LEAST GRANT ME THE MONEY I EARNED. JEANNETTE WILL DELIVER THIS...

THIS IS WORSE THAN I THOUGHT. HE WON'T SEND ANYTHING AND THREATENS TO SUE ME. GOOD THING HE DOESN'T KNOW WHERE I LIVE.

JUSTINE, COME HELP IN THE KITCHEN!

YES, MADEMOISELLE CELESTINE...

THE DOCTOR'S SISTER IS POLITE, BUT SO COLD...

I LIKE ROSALIE, THOUGH... SHE'S SUCH A DEAR!

JUSTINE, HOUSEWORK DOES NOT SUIT YOU. FROM NOW ON I WOULD LIKE YOU TO DEVOTE YOURSELF TO THE EDUCATION OF MY DAUGHTER, ROSALIE...

DON'T THINK, HOWEVER, THAT MY TRIBUTE TO YOUR VIRTUE IMPLIES THAT I PREFER IT TO VICE. VIRTUE IS NOT AN UNDENIABLE QUALITY... JUST A KIND OF BEHAVIOR, WHICH VARIES FROM PLACE TO PLACE...

NO TWO PEOPLE ON EARTH ARE VIRTUOUS IN THE SAME MANNER! THEREFORE VIRTUE HAS NO REAL BASIS, NO INHERENT GOOD. IT MUST BE USED AS A TOOL!

...HYPO-CRITICALLY ADAPTING THE MORES OF THE COUNTRY WE LIVE IN! ONLY WHAT IS USEFUL FOR ALL AGES, COUNTRIES AND PEOPLE CAN TRULY BE CONSIDERED GOOD!

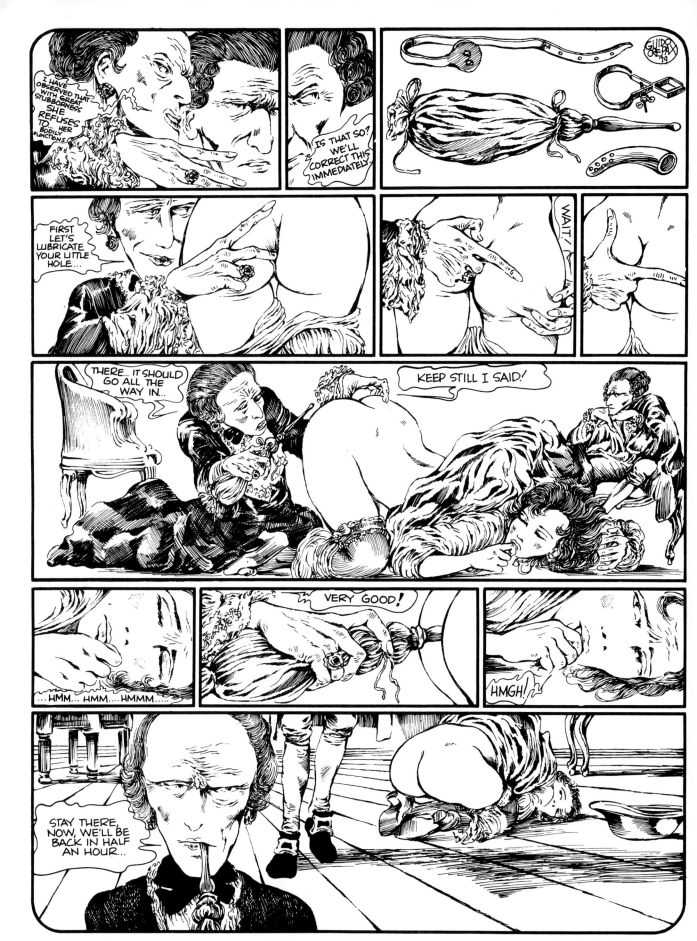

OH... THEY ENJOY TORMENT-ING ME!

OH, DARLING, I WANT TO HELP YOU...

THERE'S SOMETHING ELSE... SINCE MY MOTHER DIED... THEY...

... COME... I'LL SHOW YOU... THERE'S A CLOSET ADJOINING THEIR ROOM.

FROM THESE CRACKS YOU CAN SEE EVERY-THING.! WE'LL COME BACK...

HERE THEY ARE!

SHHH... LOOK!

TAKE THE RODS, SISTER, AND WHIP ME... YOU KNOW HOW THAT EXCITES ME!...

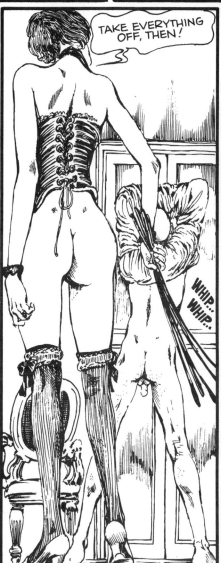

TAKE EVERYTHING OFF, THEN!

WHIP... WHIP...

HARDER, CELESTINE!

ARH!... ARH!... ARH!...

YEAH!

IT'S MY TURN, NOW... COME INTO MY ASS!

92

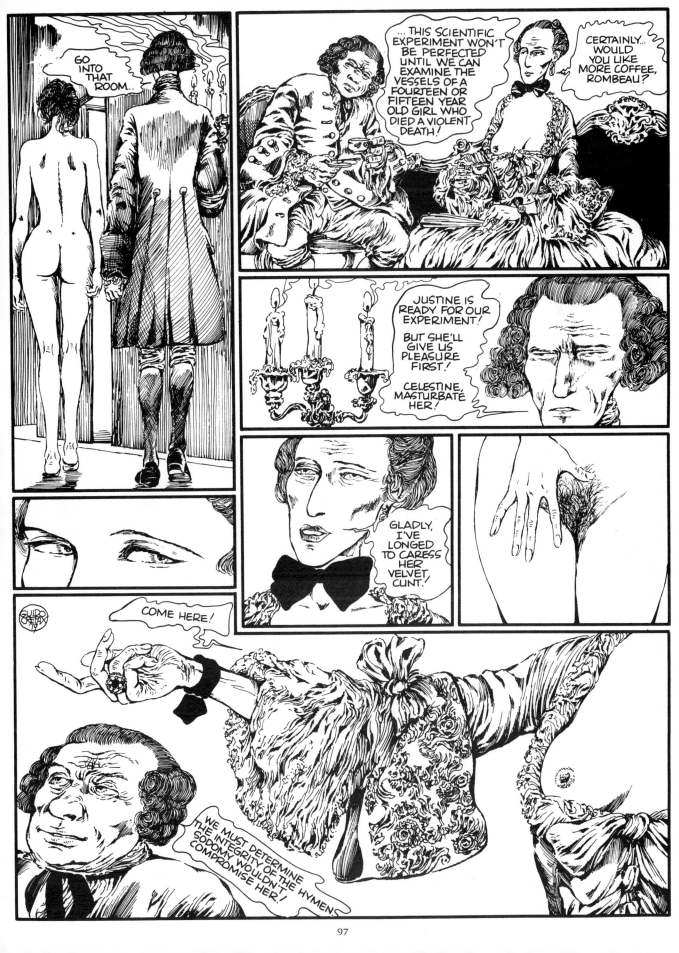

98

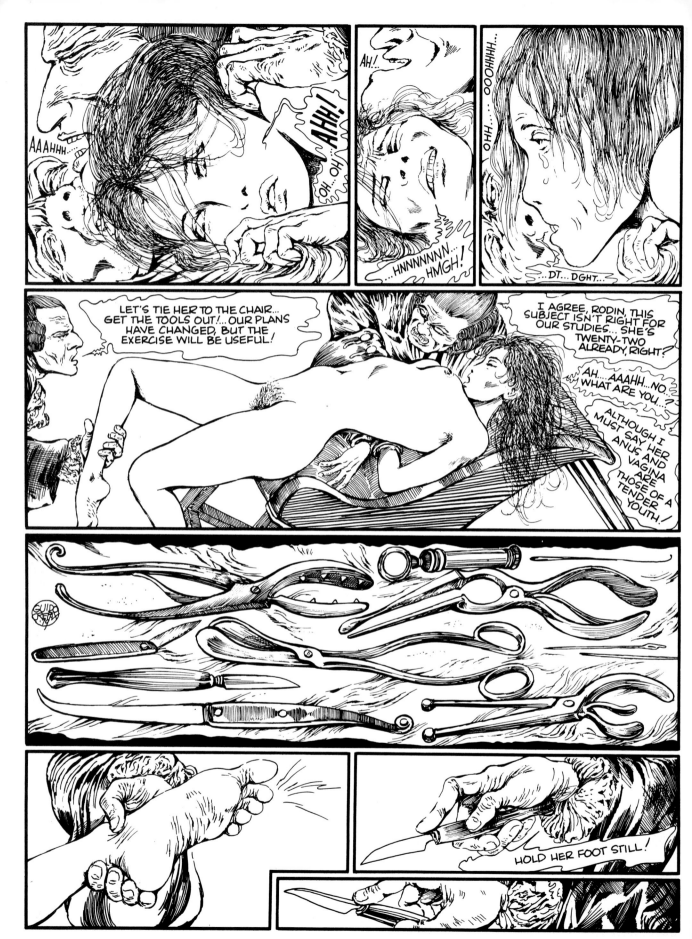

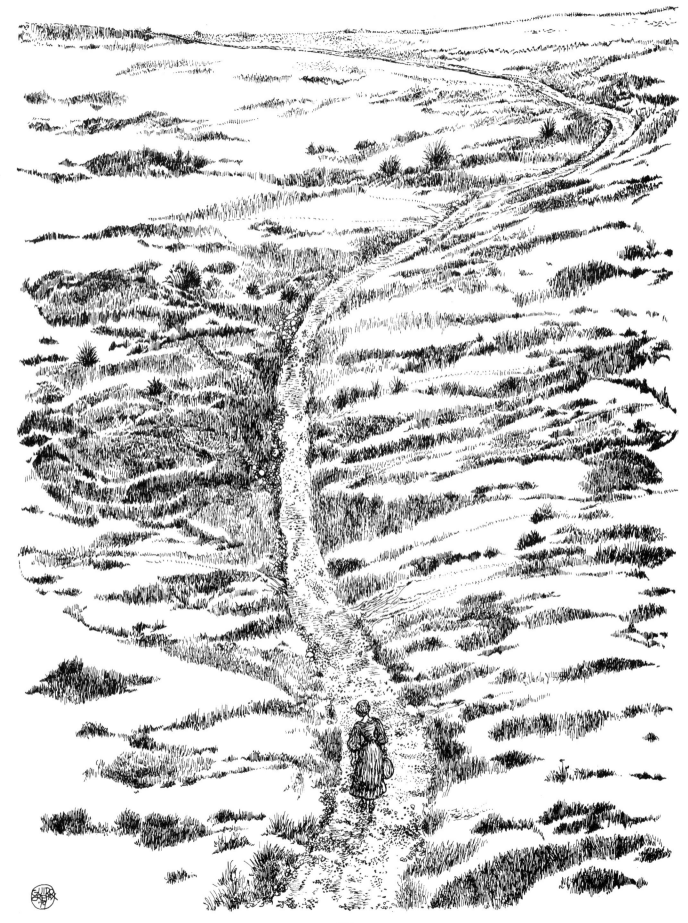

The Convent

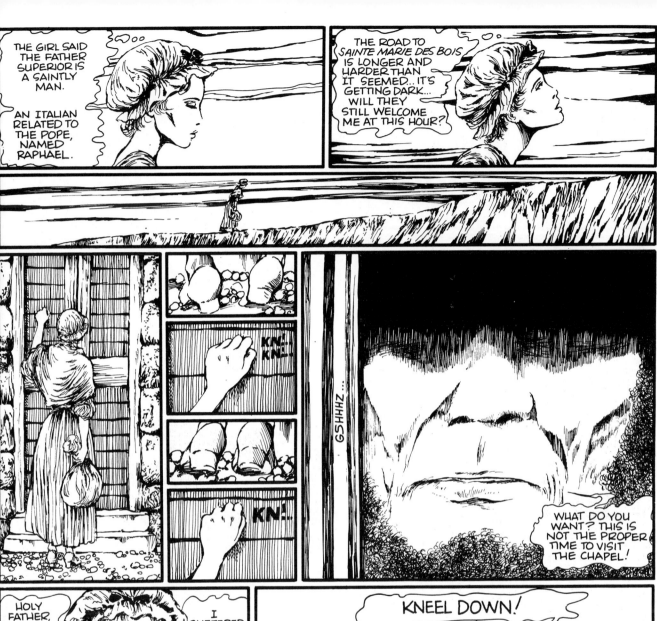

THE GIRL SAID THE FATHER SUPERIOR IS A SAINTLY MAN.

AN ITALIAN RELATED TO THE POPE, NAMED RAPHAEL.

THE ROAD TO *SAINTE MARIE DES BOIS* IS LONGER AND HARDER THAN IT SEEMED... IT'S GETTING DARK... WILL THEY STILL WELCOME ME AT THIS HOUR?

GSHHHZ...

KN! KN!..

KN!..

WHAT DO YOU WANT? THIS IS NOT THE PROPER TIME TO VISIT THE CHAPEL!

HOLY FATHER, I BEG YOU, DON'T TURN ME AWAY! I NEED...

I SUFFERED MUCH GRIEF... AND MUST CONFESS... IF YOU WOULD GIVE ME SHELTER...

KNEEL DOWN!

I AM FATHER CLEMENT, THE ADMINISTRATOR

IF YOU SEEK CONFESSION, I'LL SUMMON FATHER RAPHAEL... COME!!

I AM VERY GRATEFUL!

107

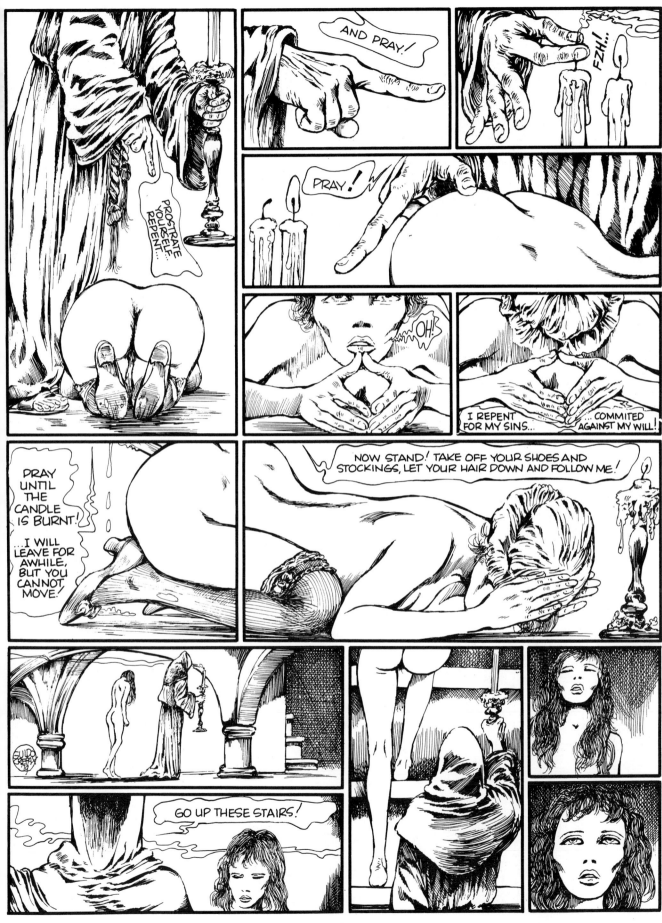

GO ON!

DRINK MORE, FLORETTE... I WANT TO BURN INCENSE ON YOUR ALTARS TONIGHT!

YOU'RE VERY QUIET TONIGHT OMPHALE!

...CORNELIE, YOUR UNPARALLELED REBELLIOUSNESS UPSETS ME GREATLY! YOU KNOW IT'S USELESS TO RESIST!

BROTHERS, I BRING YOU A NEWCOMER... SHE TELLS OF A THOUSAND MISFORTUNES... AND WHY SHOULD WE SPARE HER, SINCE THE GOD SHE PRAYS TO SO PASSIONATELY HAS USED HER ZEAL TO DELIVER HER SO SECURELY INTO OUR TRAP?

RESIGN YOURSELF TO YOUR FATE, JUSTINE... AND GIVE YOURSELF OVER TO THE IMPURE EXCESSES OF US LIBERTINES WITHOUT STRUGGLES WHICH MIGHT MAKE OUR TREATMENT OF YOU MORE DEGENERATE AND SHAMEFUL YET...

WHORE! LOVELY WHORE! I WANT HER NOW... BY GOD, I WANT TO FUCK HER!

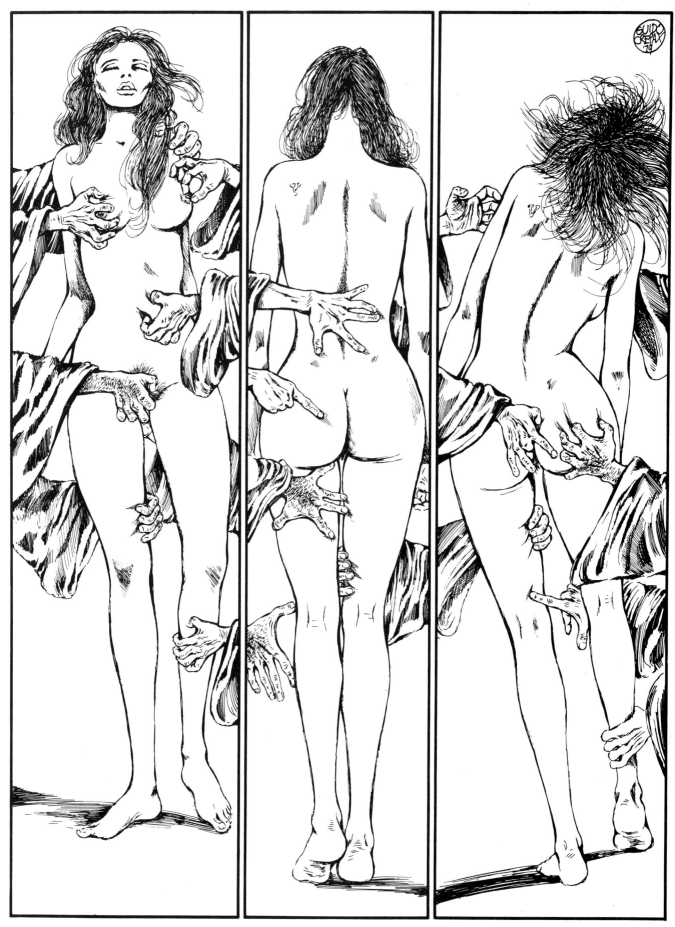

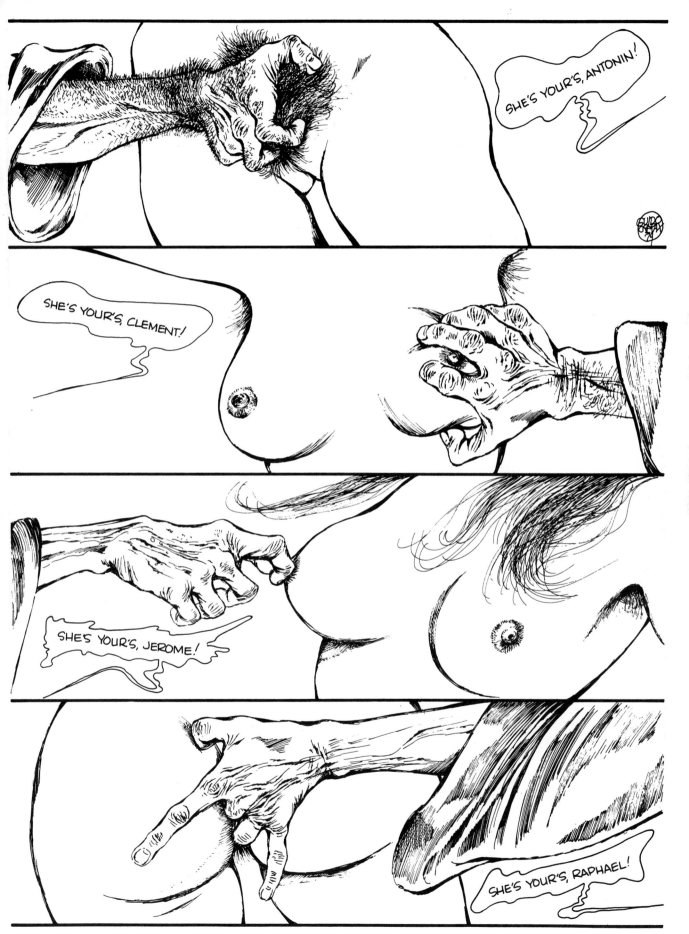

114

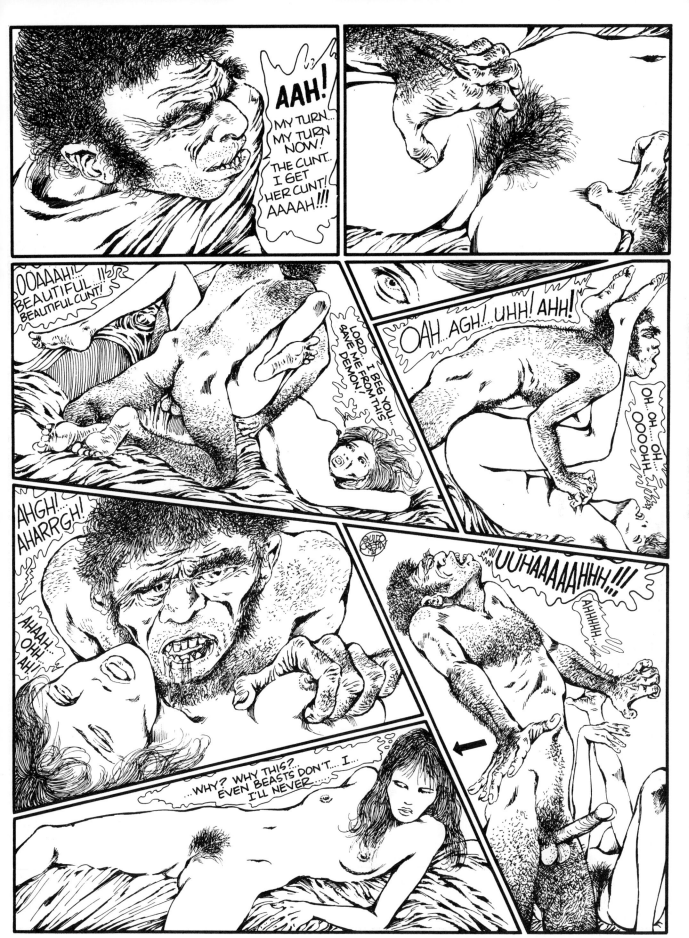

115

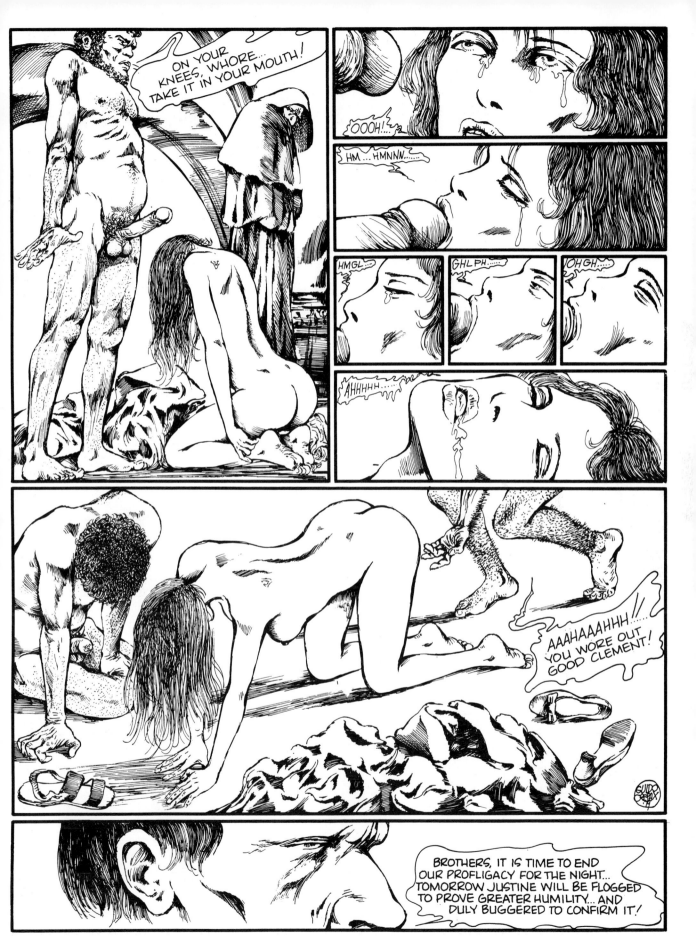

117

COME, FLORETTE... TONIGHT IT'S YOUR TURN!

GYGL...

GLSH... GLSHH... GLSHH...

LET'S GO, JUSTINE... BEFORE THOSE DEPRAVED BASTARDS CHANGE THEIR MINDS!

MY POOR FRIEND, YOU MUST BE BRAVE! LIKE YOU, I CRIED THE FIRST FEW DAYS, BUT NOW I'M USED TO IT...

...AND I HOPE THAT YOU'LL ALSO COME TO ACCEPT THAT, EVEN AS YOU REALIZE THAT OUR LOSS OF FREEDOM IS MORE PAINFUL THAN THE HUMILIATIONS THEY IMPOSE ON US...

BUT PERHAPS WE FEEL THE WORST WHEN WE THINK OF THE UNCERTAINTY OF OUR FATE.... BECAUSE IT'S IMPOSSIBLE TO KNOW WHAT WILL HAPPEN TO US WHEN WE ARE NO LONGER WANTED HERE!

WE HAVE PROOF THAT THE WOMEN RELEASED BY THE FRIARS NEVER RETURN TO THE WORLD! ALL WHO HAVE LEFT US PROMISED...

THEY SWORE THAT THEY'D REPORT THESE CRIMES... TO HAVE US FREED... BUT SO FAR WE HAVE RECEIVED NO HELP FROM THE OUTSIDE!

119

WE HAVE TO BE UP AND DRESSED BY NINE IN THE MORNING. BREAKFAST AT TEN. LUNCH AT TWO IN THE AFTERNOON. IN THE EVENING, DINNER, AND THE ORGIES... HERE, THERE ARE NO RULES... EXCEPT TO REFUSE NOTHING... ...BE READY FOR ANYTHING!

ANOTHER THING... AT FIVE P.M. THE REGENT VISITS US... HE LISTENS TO MY REPORT... GOES THROUGH OUR QUARTERS AND OBSERVES. HE SELDOM LEAVES WITHOUT HAVING HIS FUN WITH AT LEAST ONE OF US... OR ALL FOUR!

YOU'LL SOON MEET THE CREATURE WHO CLEANS OUR ROOMS, AN OLD FRIAR. HE'S NEARLY BLIND, CRIPPLED AND MUTE. HE TAKES CARE OF THE HOUSEKEEPING WITH THREE OTHERS.

SOMETIMES WE RECEIVE UNANNOUNCED VISITS. ON THOSE OCCASIONS WE PERFORM CEREMONIES WHICH YOU WILL LEARN BY HEART, UNDER THE THREAT OF PUNISHMENT...

THAT'S ALL I CAN TELL YOU, BUT DON'T DESPAIR IF THAT'S POSSIBLE. YOU HAVE TO FORGET THE OUTSIDE WORLD... NONE OF THE WOMEN IN THIS HOUSE WILL EVER SEE IT AGAIN!

BUT I WANT TO KNOW MORE ...TELL ME! DO YOU REALLY BELIEVE THAT WE'LL NEVER...?

I ONLY KNOW WHAT I HAVE TOLD YOU... WHEN ONE OF US LEAVES, SHE NEVER REAPPEARS... I NOTICED, THOUGH, THAT AT THOSE TIMES, THE MONKS EAT VERY LITTLE... THEY DRINK PLENTY AND DON'T KEEP US OVERNIGHT...

MY DEAR FRIEND, SHALL WE MAKE A PACT? ON MY PART I SWEAR THAT IF I DO NOT DIE HERE, I WILL SOMEHOW PUT AN END TO THIS INFAMY! DO YOU PROMISE THE SAME?

OF COURSE I SWEAR.

120

OMPHALE HAS GONE SO AS TO LET ME SLEEP. BUT MY THOUGHTS WILL KEEP ME AWAKE...

I THINK I KNOW!... YES, I THINK I KNOW WHAT END AWAITS US HERE...

...WE'LL BE TAKEN TO THE DUNGEONS, WHERE...

...THEY WILL CHOP OUR HEADS OFF...

AND THEY WILL EAT US!

122

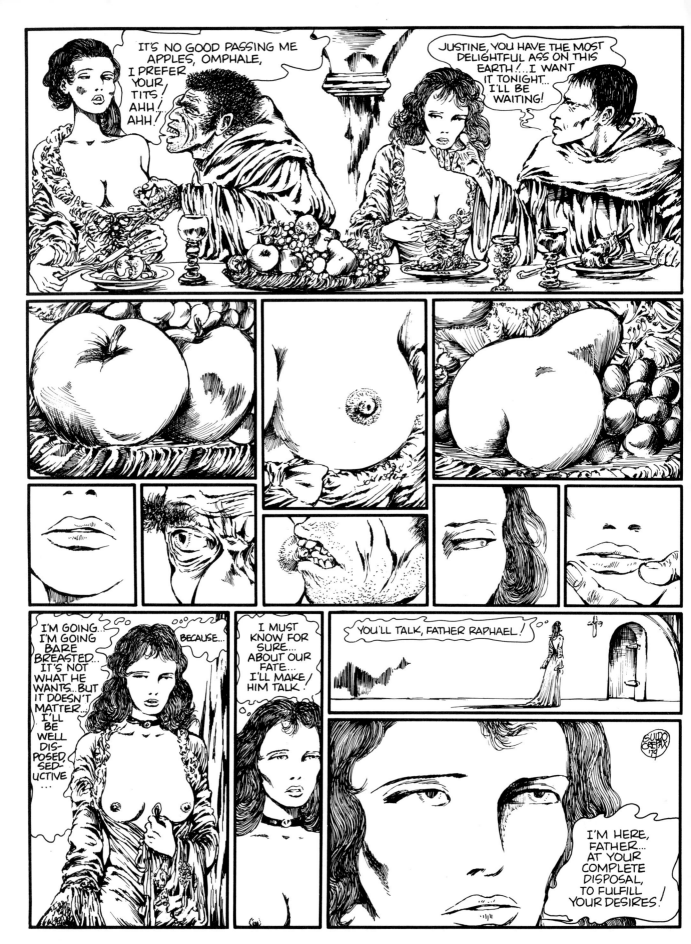

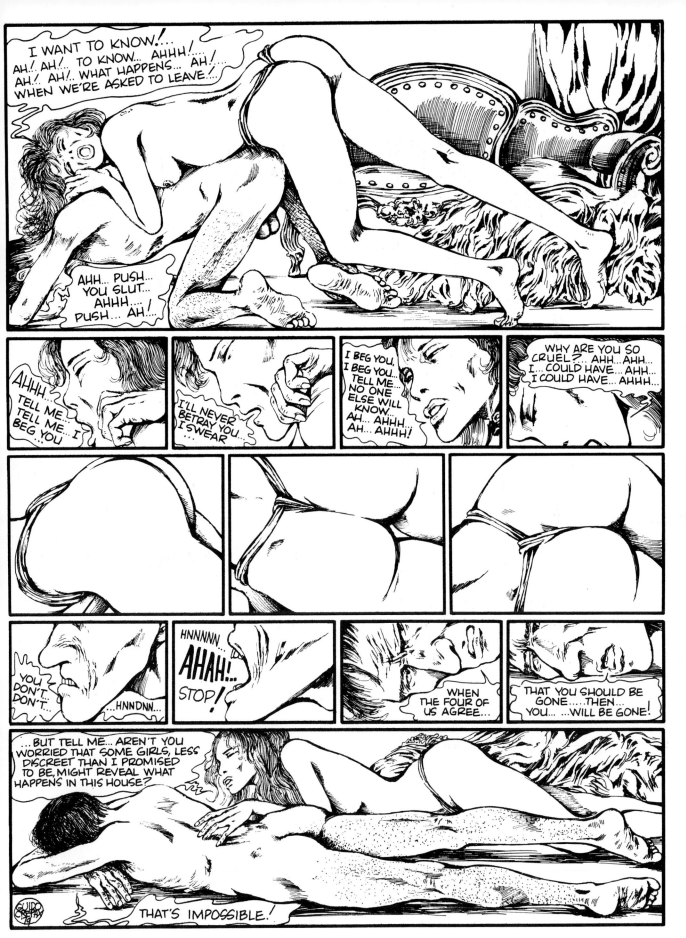

129

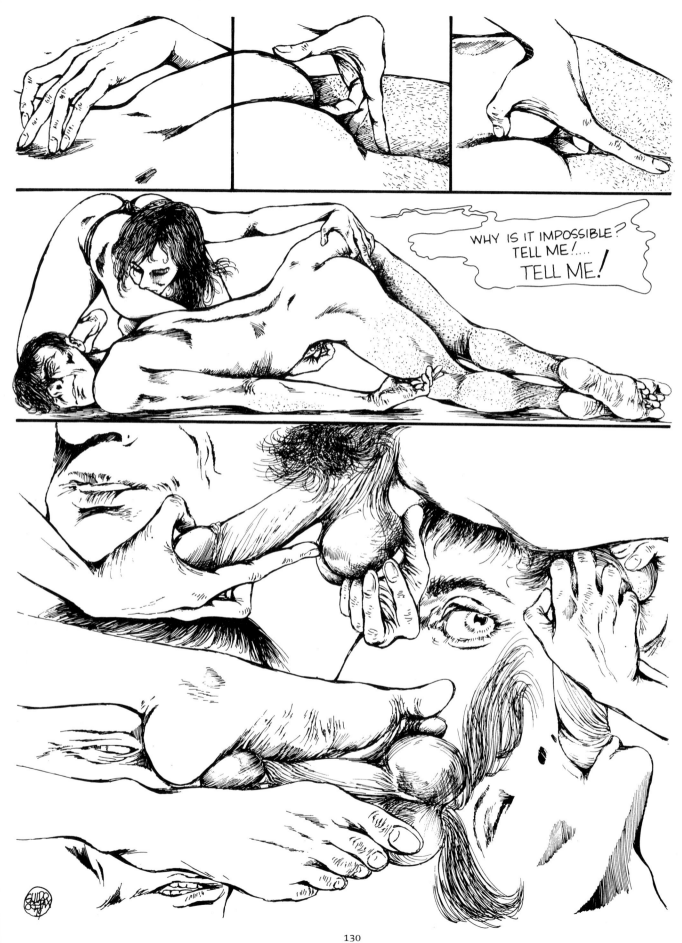

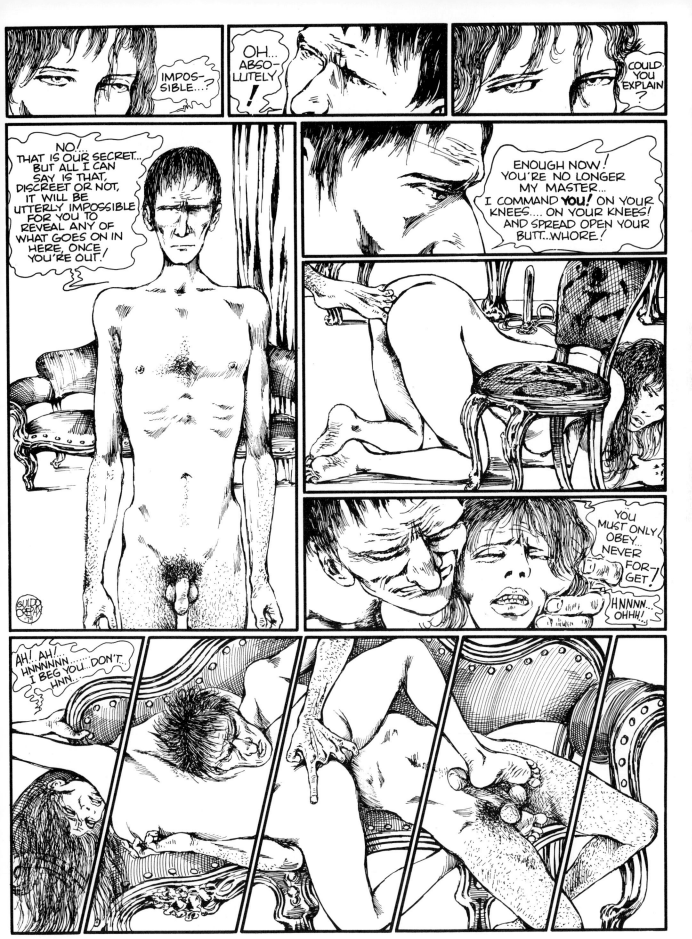

WHAT ABOUT THE RISK OF PREGNANCY? DON'T YOU WORRY ABOUT THAT

YOU MUST HAVE REALIZED THAT ONLY FATHER ANTONIN PLACES US IN THAT DANGER, AND HE GIVES US HERBAL INFUSIONS. THEY'RE MIRACULOUSLY EFFECTIVE

OH!.. FATHER RAPHAEL!

I WANT THE FOUR OF YOU ON ALL FOURS!

IT'S MY TIME... I KNOW IT...

CORNELIE... FLORETTE... OMPHALE... JUSTINE... ... OMPHALE...

OMPHALE!

YOU HAVE SERVED LONG ENOUGH... WE REPUDIATE YOU!

YOU ARE TO SPEND NAKED EXCEPT I WILL AT NIGHTFALL...

THE DAY COMPLETELY FOR YOUR SHOES. SUMMON YOU

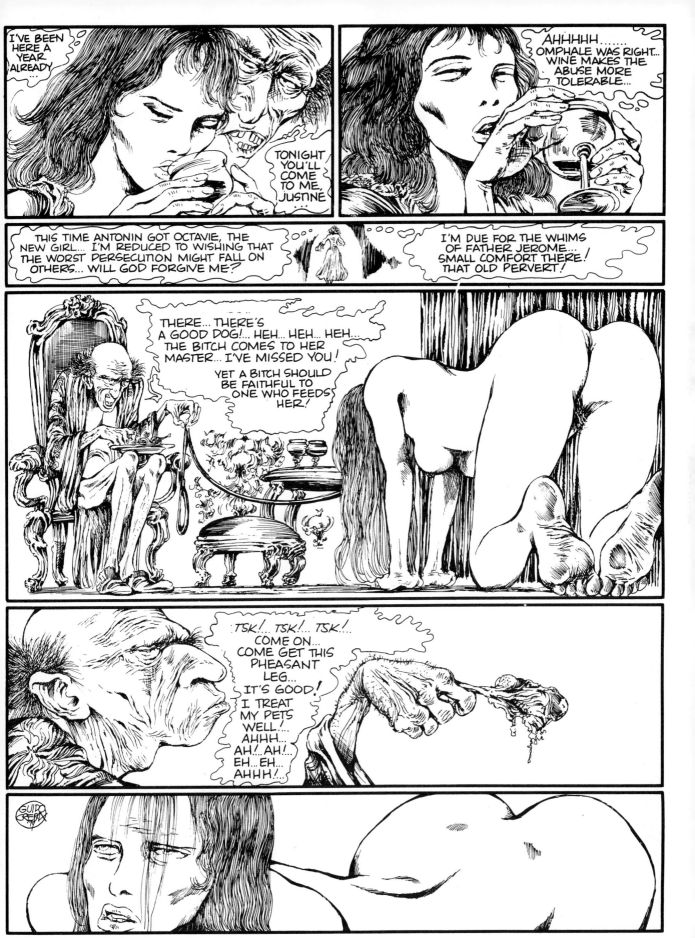

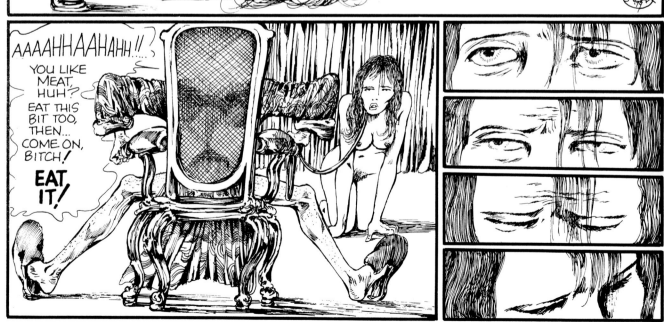

136

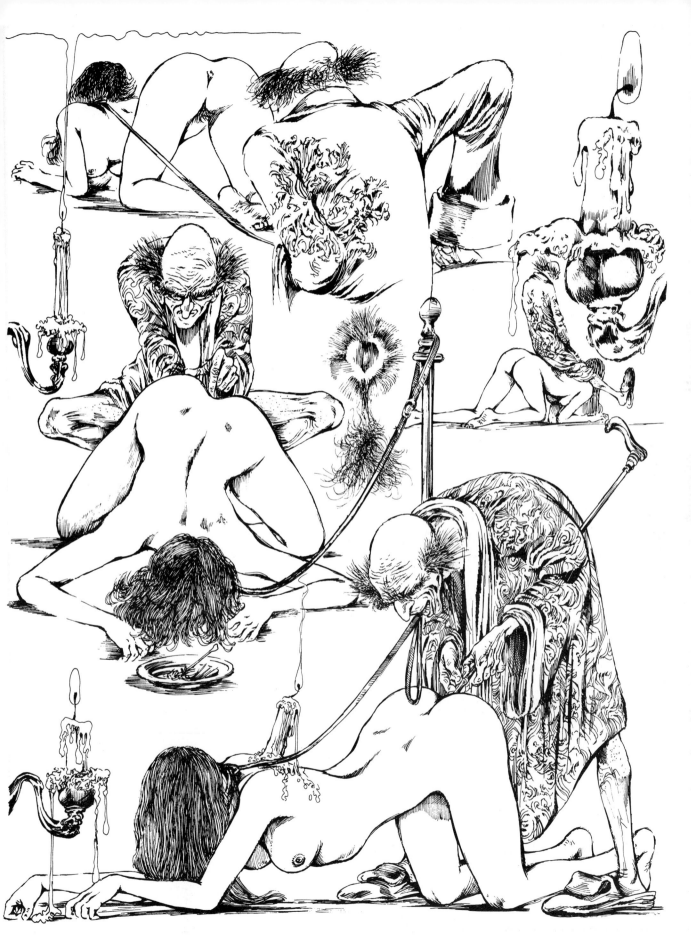

139

Dalville

I'LL REST A BIT HERE IN LYON... WHAT?! I CAN'T BELIEVE THIS NEWS!... DOCTOR RODIN HAS BEEN APPOINTED SURGEON GENERAL FOR THE COURT OF THE KING OF SWEDEN!

IT SEEMS TRUE, THEN, THAT FORTUNE PREFERS EVIL... BUT I WILL NEVER BELIEVE IT... IT WOULD MEAN PLACING THE DEVIL ABOVE GOD!

I'VE CHOSEN MY ROAD...

PLEASE HAVE MERCY ON A POOR SOUL. YOU'LL BE REWARDED!

HERE'S A GOLD COIN, DEAR WOMAN....

GIVE ME THAT, BIRDBRAIN!

AH!

SDUN!...

GOOD JOB! LET'S GO!

...OWW... OWWW... I'M HURT! THAT WITCH IS STRONGER THAN SHE LOOKS... AND NOW SHE'S RUNNING OFF WITH HER GROUP... HOW CAN FATE KEEP PUNISHING MY GOOD INTENTIONS?

WHAT'S GOING ON THERE?

YOU WANTED TO CHEAT US, HUH? TAKE THIS!

SCOUNDRELS! YOU'LL KILL ME!

143

144

146

147

OH!.... AAH!

STZREEK!..STZLACHK:

WHIP...

TAKE THIS! JUST AS A REMINDER TO BE OBEDIENT!

AT NIGHT YOU'LL SLEEP IN THESE CELLS. YOU'LL GET WATER, BREAD AND SOME BEANS.

THEY LAUGHED.... THEY LAUGHED AT ME AS THEY WHIPPED... HMGH..... THESE MEN ENJOY THE SUFFERING OF OTHERS... AND NOT IN THE HEAT OF PASSION! IT'S PURE CRUELTY.

GHSHD...

THEY EXIST ONLY TO TORMENT OTHERS... THEY'RE NOT HUMAN.

MY GOD! WHAT NOW?

GHZSH...

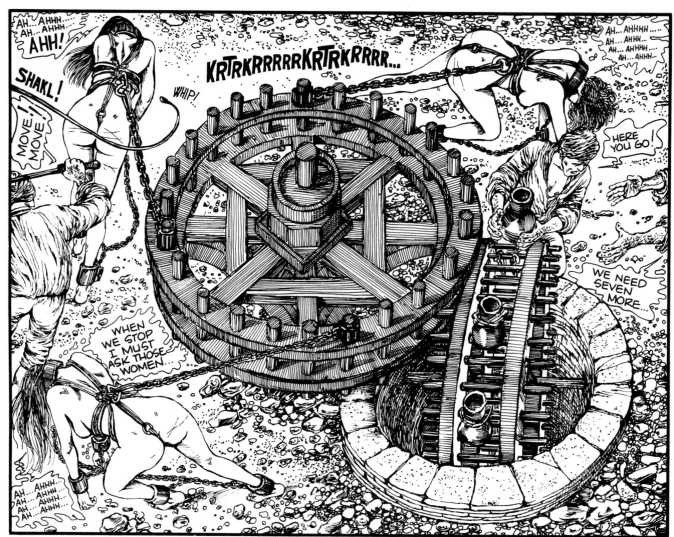

AH... AHHH...
AH... AHHH...
AHH!

SHAKL!

WHIP!

KRTRKRRRRRKRTRKRRRR...

MOVE! MOVE!

AH... AHHH...
AH... AHHH...
AH... AHHH...
AH... AHHH...

HERE YOU GO!

WE NEED SEVEN MORE.

WHEN WE STOP I MUST ASK THOSE WOMEN

AH... AHHH...
AH... AHHH...
AH... AHHH...

I WAS DALVILLE'S LOVER... I WAS RICH, REVERED... UNTIL THAT MONSTER BROUGHT ME HERE!.. JUST LIKE THE NEXT ONE.

NOW HE HAS ANOTHER LOVER... LUCKY WOMAN... SHE'LL FOLLOW HIM TO VENICE AND ENJOY THE FRUITS OF HIS CRIMES.

OH... OHH...
OH... OHH...
OH... OHH...

AAAH!...

WHIP!

SHLAZ!

GET TO WORK! PUT THOSE LAZY BONES BACK TO WORK! ENOUGH REST!

NO!

150

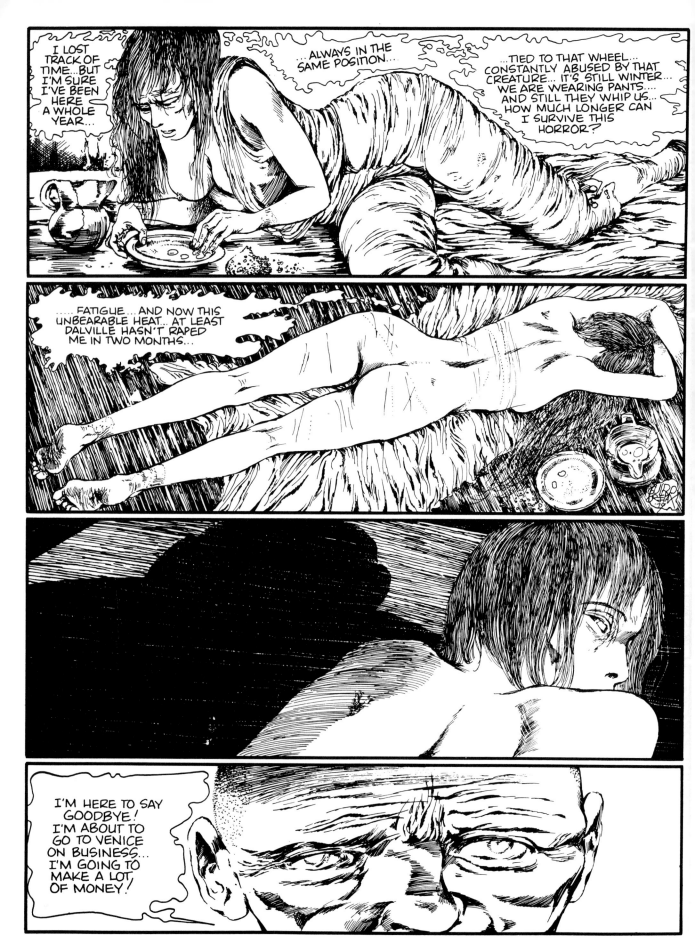

I LOST TRACK OF TIME...BUT I'M SURE I'VE BEEN HERE A WHOLE YEAR...

...ALWAYS IN THE SAME POSITION...

...TIED TO THAT WHEEL... CONSTANTLY ABUSED BY THAT CREATURE... IT'S STILL WINTER... WE ARE WEARING PANTS.... AND STILL THEY WHIP US... HOW MUCH LONGER CAN I SURVIVE THIS HORROR?

...FATIGUE... AND NOW THIS UNBEARABLE HEAT... AT LEAST DALVILLE HASN'T RAPED ME IN TWO MONTHS...

I'M HERE TO SAY GOODBYE! I'M ABOUT TO GO TO VENICE ON BUSINESS... I'M GOING TO MAKE A LOT OF MONEY!

153

155

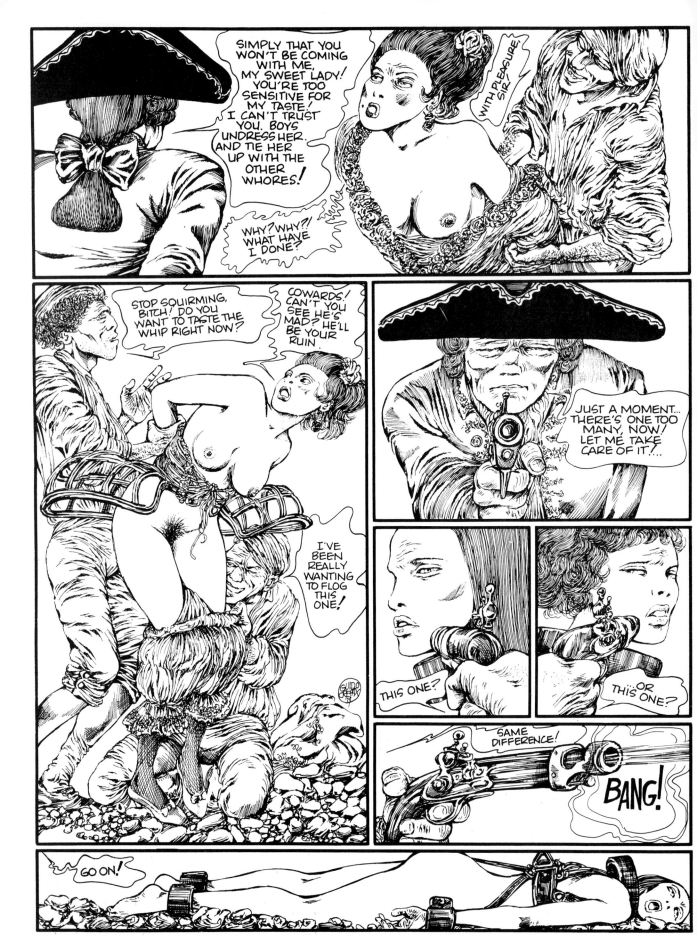

156

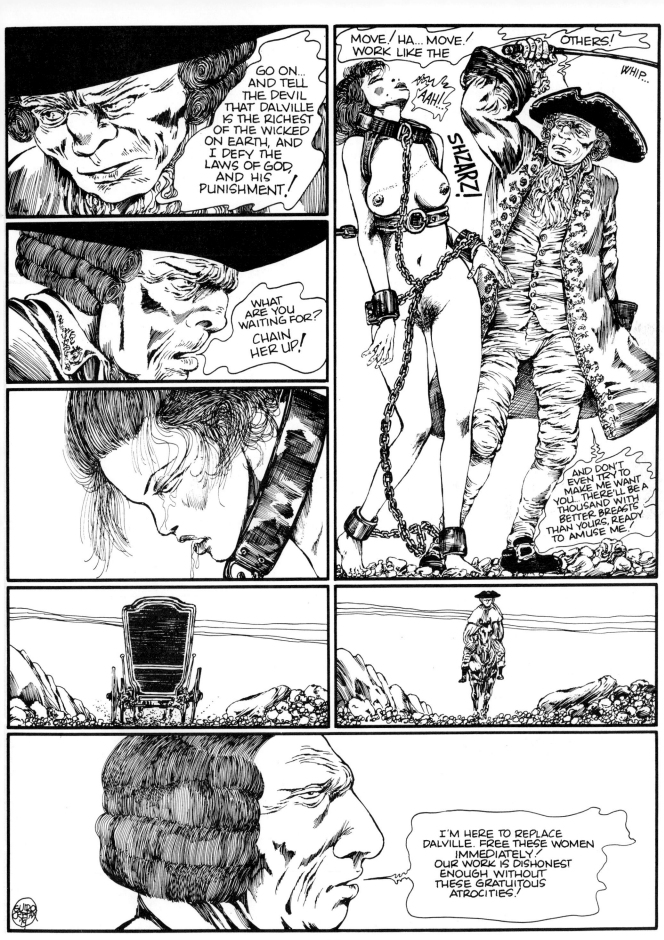

Epilogue

WHAT ABOUT FEAR OF GOD? DON'T YOU BELIEVE THAT, IN A BETTER WORLD, DIVINE JUSTICE AWAITS CALLOUS SINNERS?

IF GOD EXISTED THERE SHOULD BE LESS SUFFERING ON THIS WORLD! SINCE THERE IS EVIL ON EARTH IT MUST BE MADE POSSIBLE BY YOUR GOD... EITHER THAT OR HE HAS NO POWER TO STOP IT!... I WON'T LOVE A CRUEL GOD OR A WEAK ONE!

BUT ENOUGH PHILOSOPHY! I NEED A FAVOR. PLEASE DON'T REFUSE ME! I'LL PAY YOU A HUNDRED LOUIS IF THINGS WORK OUT. HAVE YOU NOTICED THE YOUNG MAN WHO'S BEEN DINING AT OUR TABLE FOR THE LAST THREE DAYS?

YOU MEAN DUBREUIL?

PRECISELY! WELL, HE'S IN LOVE WITH YOU! HE CONFESSED IT TO ME HIMSELF. AND I CAN'T BLAME HIM, YOU'RE SO PRETTY!

OOH!

THE POINT IS DUBREUIL IS A RICH MERCHANT. HE KEEPS SIX-HUNDRED THOUSAND FRANCS IN HIS ROOM. I'LL SET UP A CARRIAGE RIDE FOR THE TWO OF YOU... YOU CAN EASILY DISTRACT HIM FOR AS LONG AS I NEED... AFTER I ROB HIM I'LL STAY IN THE HOTEL SO HE WON'T SUSPECT ME!

PFF... SHE HASN'T CHANGED AT ALL. THE BEST THING TO DO IS TO PRETEND I'M GOING ALONG WITH IT... OTHERWISE...

ALL RIGHT, I'LL DO WHAT YOU ASK! BUT I ACCEPT ONLY BECAUSE I'M IN NEED.

STILL, YOU AREN'T OFFERING VERY MUCH. I COULD MAKE MORE BY SELLING MYSELF TO DUBREUIL.

HA! HA! HA! I SEE YOU'VE GOTTEN CLEVER... CONGRATULATIONS! HERE'S AN I.O.U. FOR A THOUSAND LOUIS!

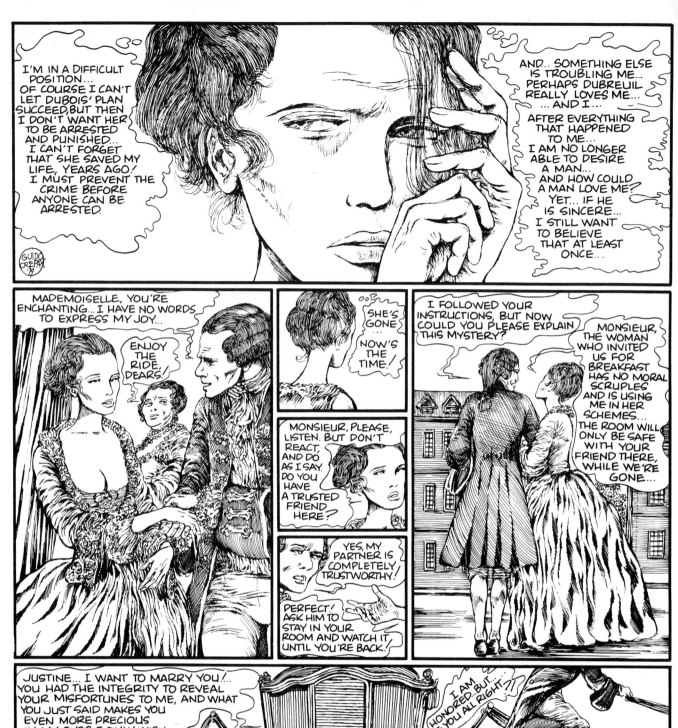

AAAHHH....AHH!!!

NOOOO!!!.....

CURSE YOU! YOU SHOULD HAVE LEFT HER IN THE ROOM. THE FIRE DIDN'T GET THERE!

AH... HOW COULD I KNOW...

EVERYTHING'S BEEN STOLEN! EVERYTHING! AHH! I'M RUINED... ...AHAAH!!

THAT HYPOCRITE! SHE ONLY THOUGHT OF SAVING HERSELF, AND NOW SHE MOURNS HER MONEY MORE THAN HER DAUGHTER!

IT'S HER FAULT! IT'S ALL JUSTINE'S FAULT! I SHOULD HAVE KNOWN... SHE RAN FROM GRENOBLE UNDER SUSPICION OF MURDER... AND IN LYON A FRIAR TOLD ME OF HER SINS!

I'M LOST! THERE'S NO HOPE... I'VE BEEN CHARGED WITH THEFT, ARSON AND INFANTICIDE.

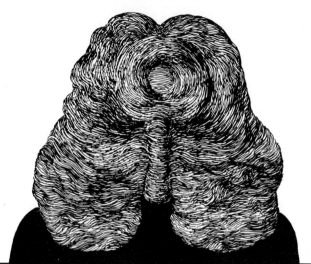

TRIALS ARE SWIFT AFFAIRS IN THE LOWER COURTS. THE SENTENCE IS PASSED BY IDIOTS WHO GO BY THE BOOK OR BRUTAL FANATICS. THE JURY, COMPOSED OF SHOPKEEPERS SAFE IN LETTING HIGHER RANK CORRECT THEIR MISTAKES, EMITS IT'S VERDICT...

GUILTY!

THIS IS MY STORY EXACTLY AS IT HAPPENED...

NOW I'LL BE TAKEN TO PARIS FOR CONFIRMATION OR REFUSAL OF THE SENTENCE... I HAVE NO ILLUSIONS...

170

AND SO MADAME LORSANGE AND HER LOVER DELIGHTED THEMSELVES IN EFFORTS TO BRING JUSTINE FROM THE DEPTHS OF MISFORTUNE TO THE GREATEST HEIGHTS OF COMFORT AND PROSPERITY. USING ALL THE SUBLETY THAT COULD BE EXPECTED FROM TWO SENSITIVE SOULS...

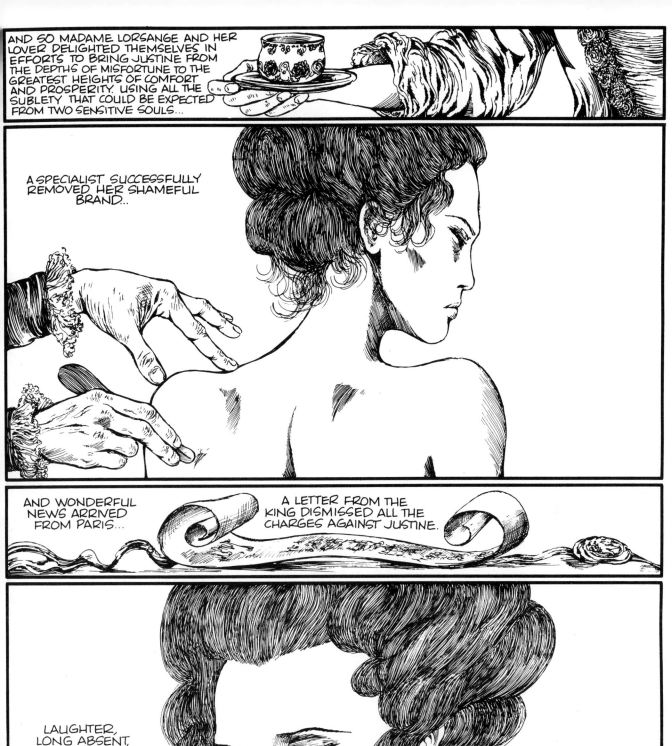

A SPECIALIST SUCCESSFULLY REMOVED HER SHAMEFUL BRAND...

AND WONDERFUL NEWS ARRIVED FROM PARIS...

A LETTER FROM THE KING DISMISSED ALL THE CHARGES AGAINST JUSTINE.

LAUGHTER, LONG ABSENT, ONCE AGAIN GRACED HER LIPS...

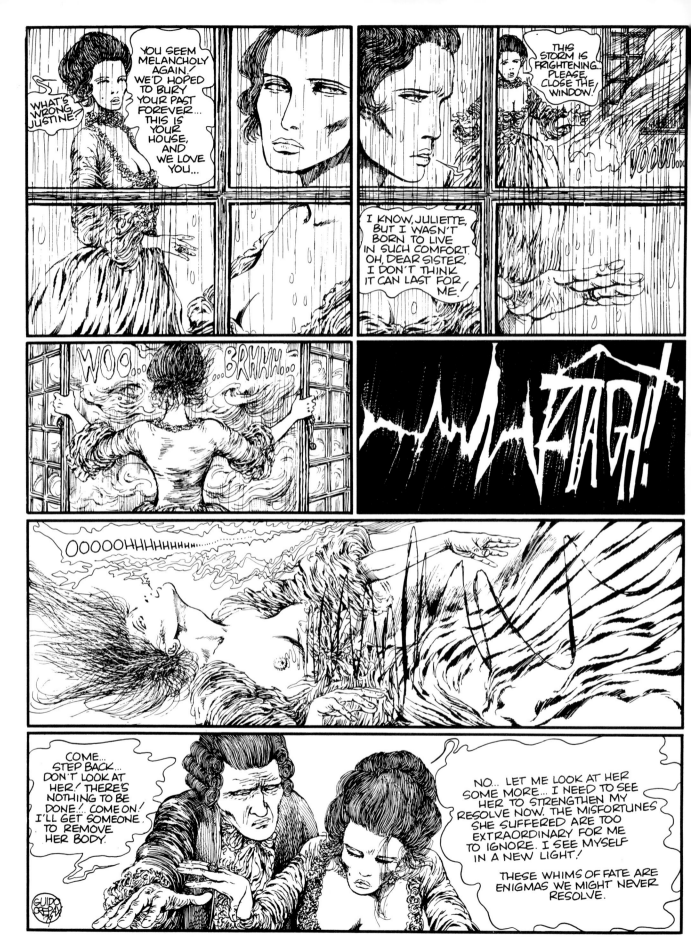

172

MADAME LORSANGE LEFT HER HOME IMMEDIATELY AND RAN TO PARIS, WHERE SHE JOINED THE ORDER OF THE CARMELITE NUNS...

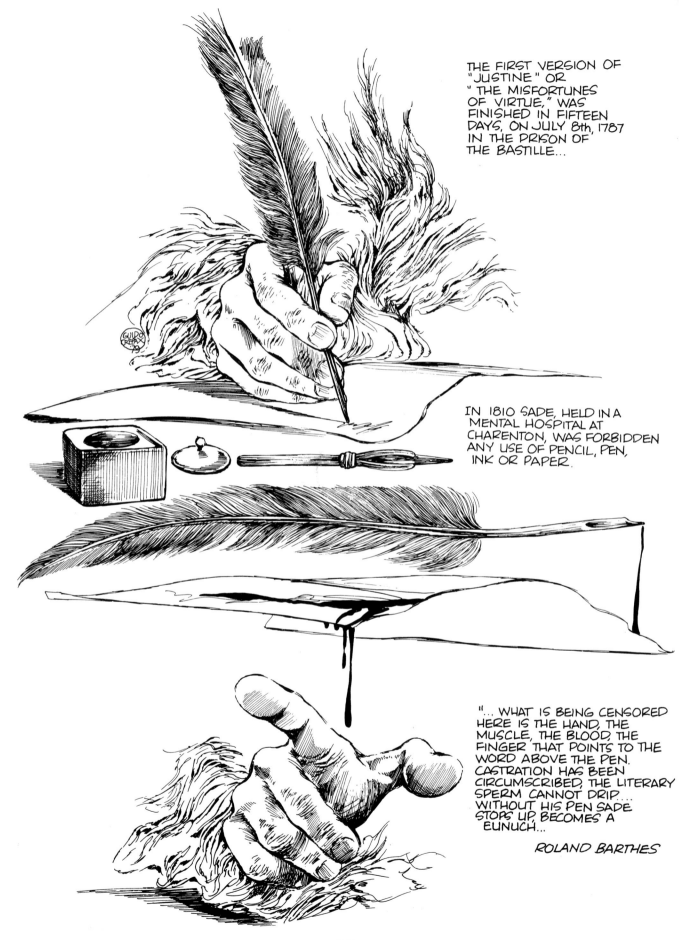

THE FIRST VERSION OF "JUSTINE" OR "THE MISFORTUNES OF VIRTUE," WAS FINISHED IN FIFTEEN DAYS, ON JULY 8th, 1787 IN THE PRISON OF THE BASTILLE...

IN 1810 SADE, HELD IN A MENTAL HOSPITAL AT CHARENTON, WAS FORBIDDEN ANY USE OF PENCIL, PEN, INK OR PAPER.

"... WHAT IS BEING CENSORED HERE IS THE HAND, THE MUSCLE, THE BLOOD, THE FINGER THAT POINTS TO THE WORD ABOVE THE PEN. CASTRATION HAS BEEN CIRCUMSCRIBED, THE LITERARY SPERM CANNOT DRIP... WITHOUT HIS PEN SADE STOPS UP, BECOMES A EUNUCH...

ROLAND BARTHES

The Story of O

The Lovers
of Roissy

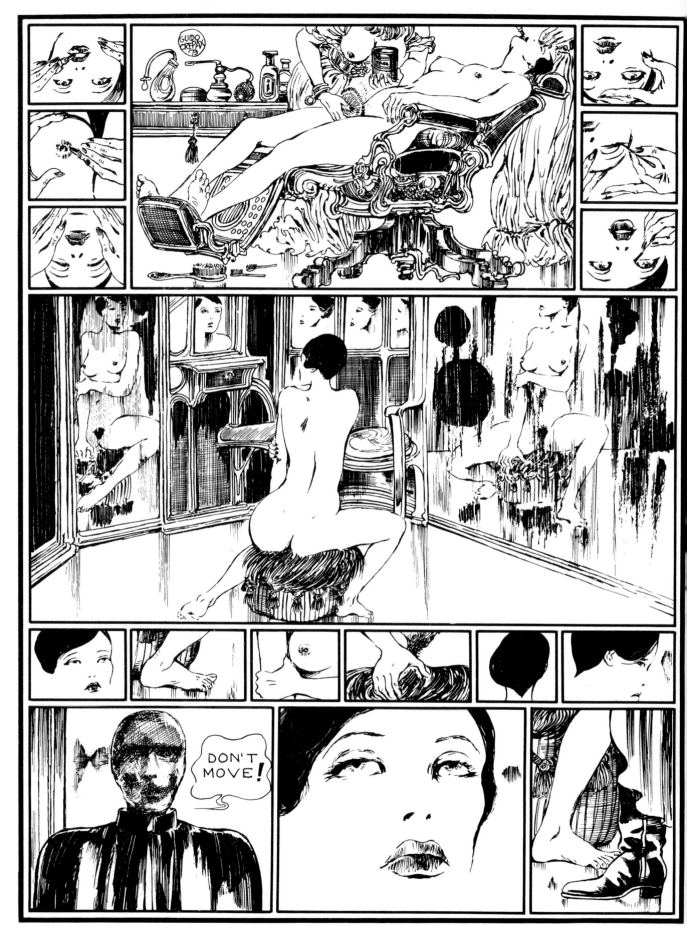

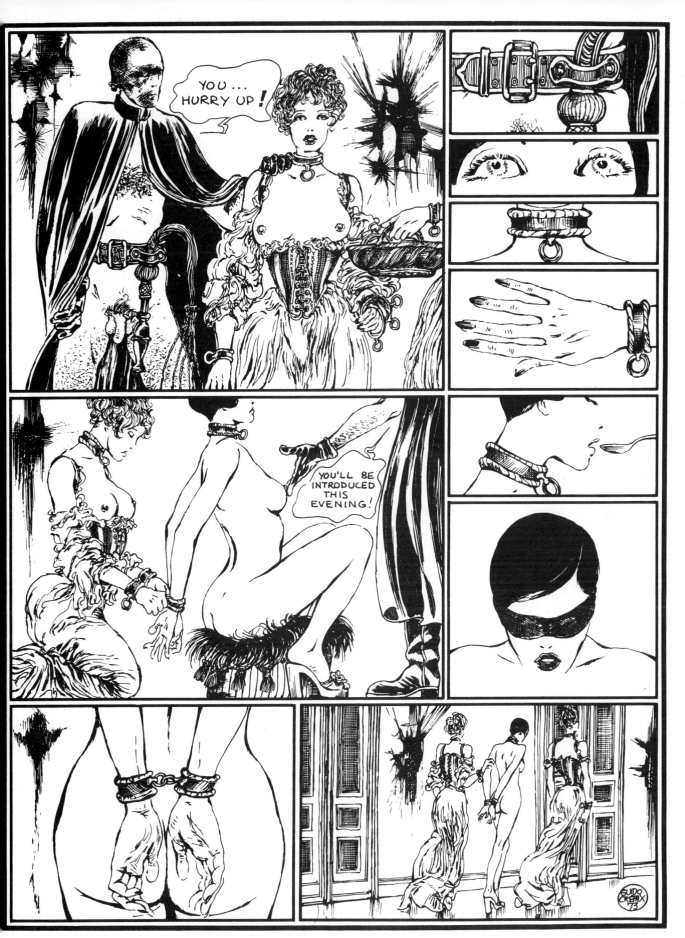

AH!

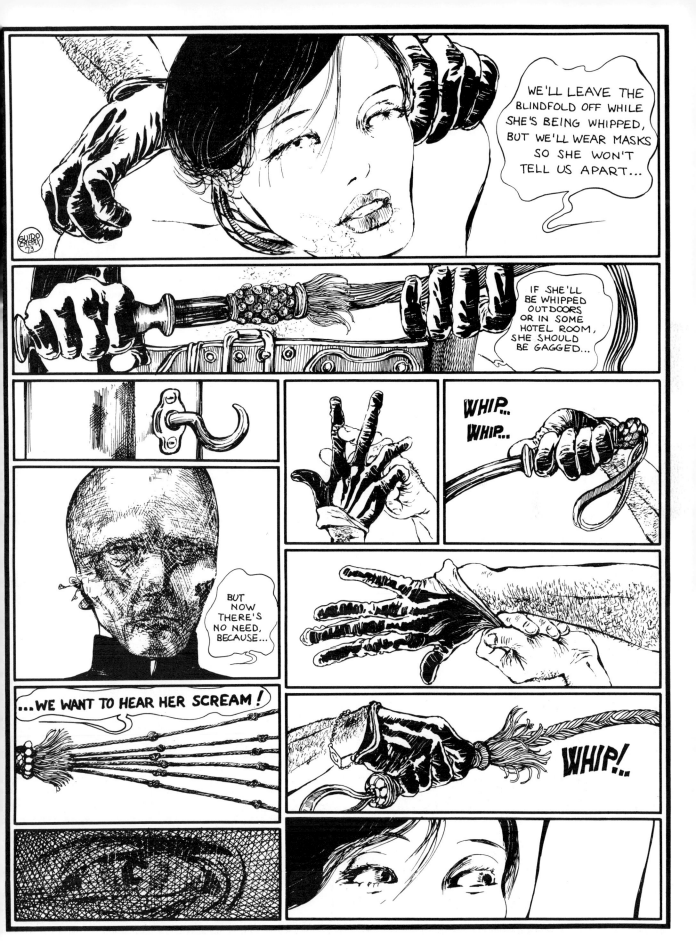

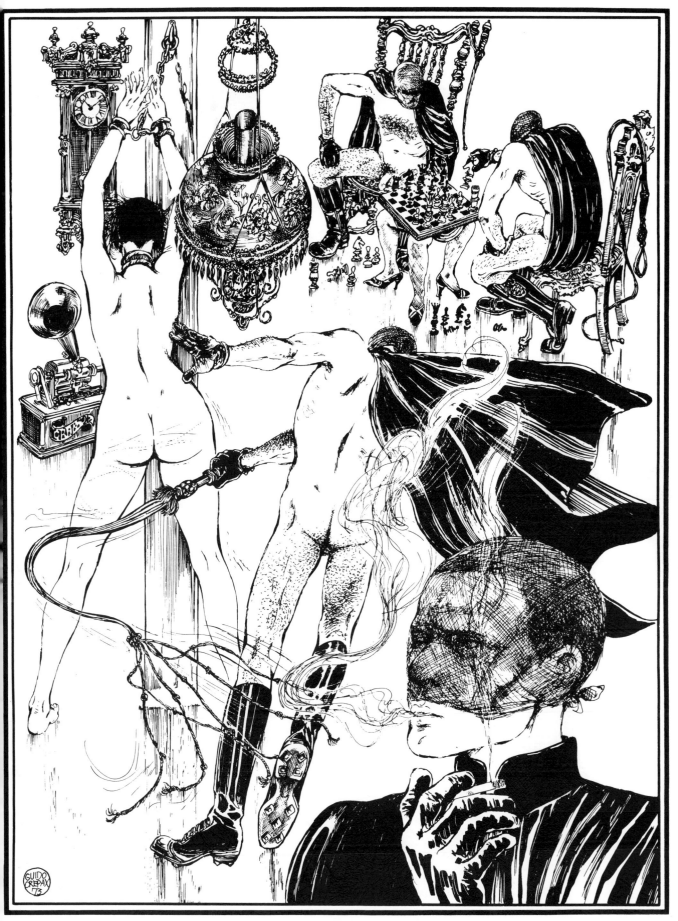

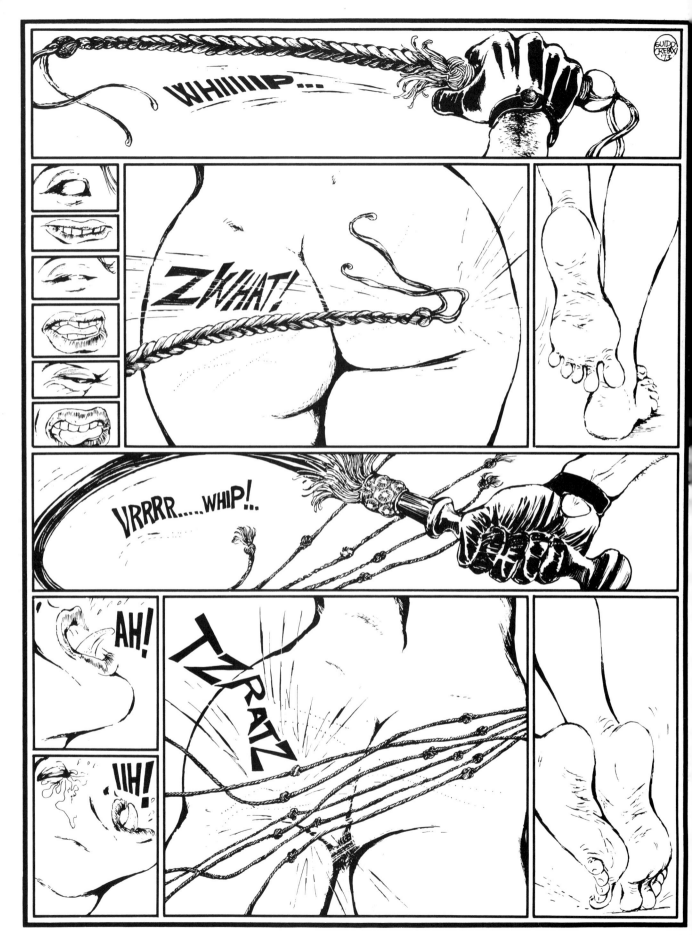

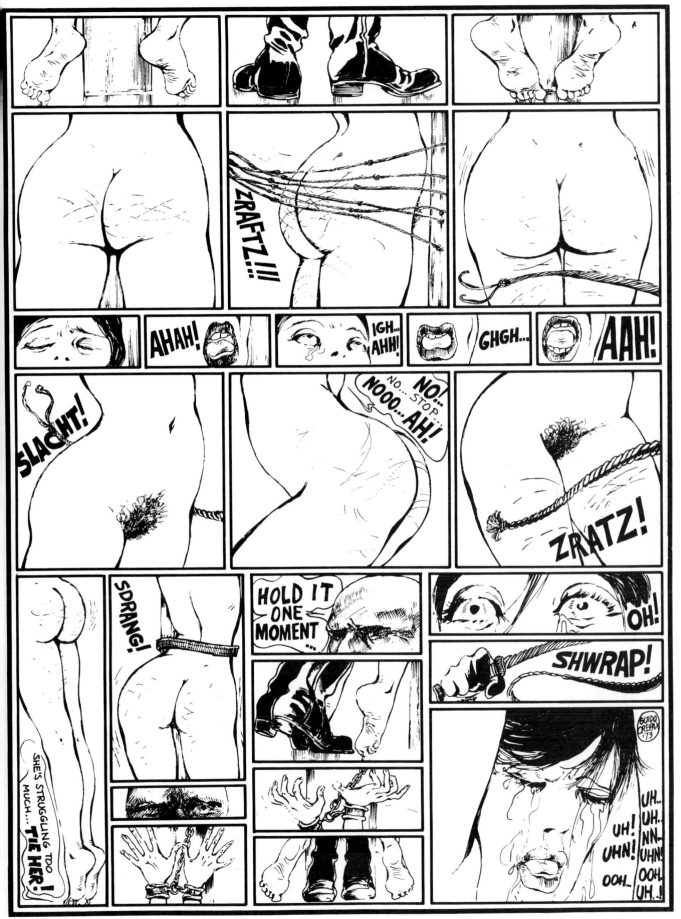

193

DRLNG!..
DRLNG!..

IN OUR
PRESENCE
YOUR LIPS
WILL
ALWAYS
BE PARTED
...

YOU WILL LIFT YOUR
SKIRTS WHEN ORDERED
TO DO SO...

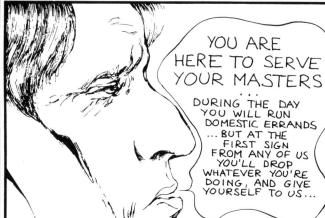

YOU ARE
HERE TO SERVE
YOUR MASTERS
...
DURING THE DAY
YOU WILL RUN
DOMESTIC ERRANDS
...BUT AT THE
FIRST SIGN
FROM ANY OF US
YOU'LL DROP
WHATEVER YOU'RE
DOING, AND GIVE
YOURSELF TO US...

...AND
YOU WON'T
CROSS
YOUR LEGS...
OR PRESS
YOUR KNEES
TOGETHER...

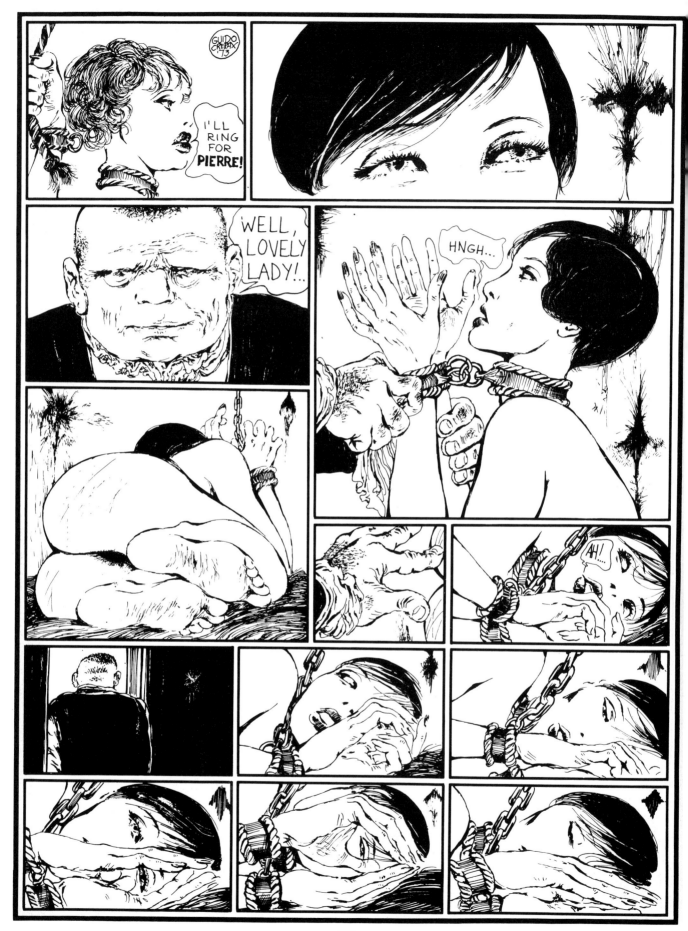

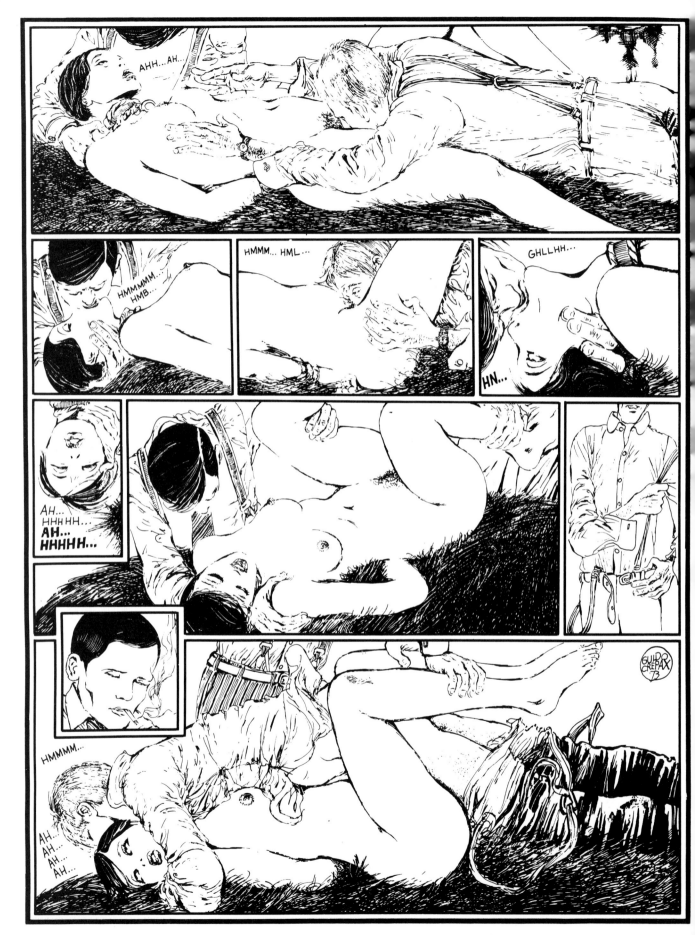

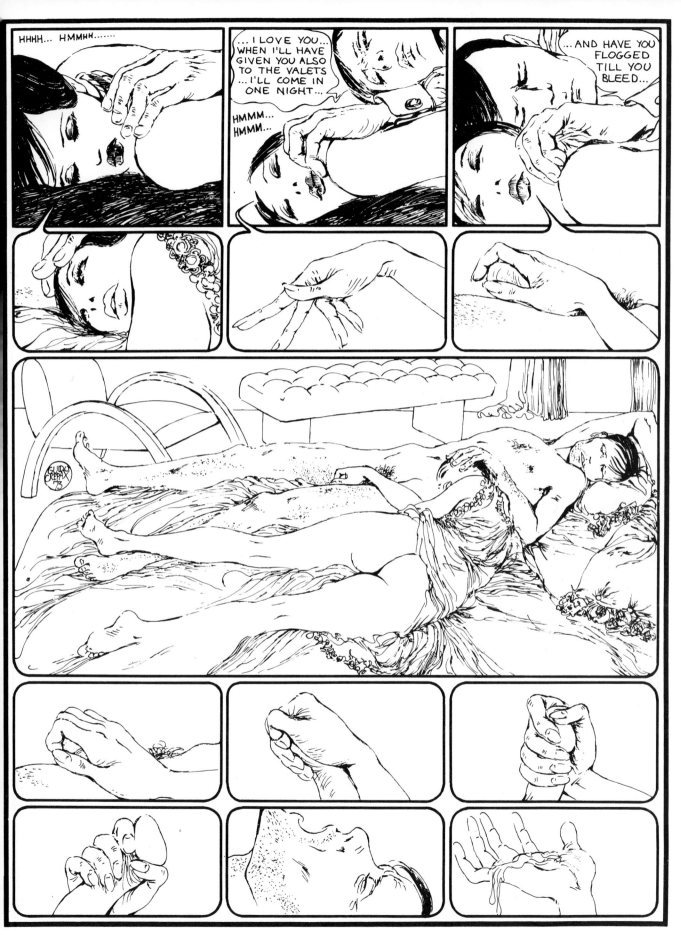

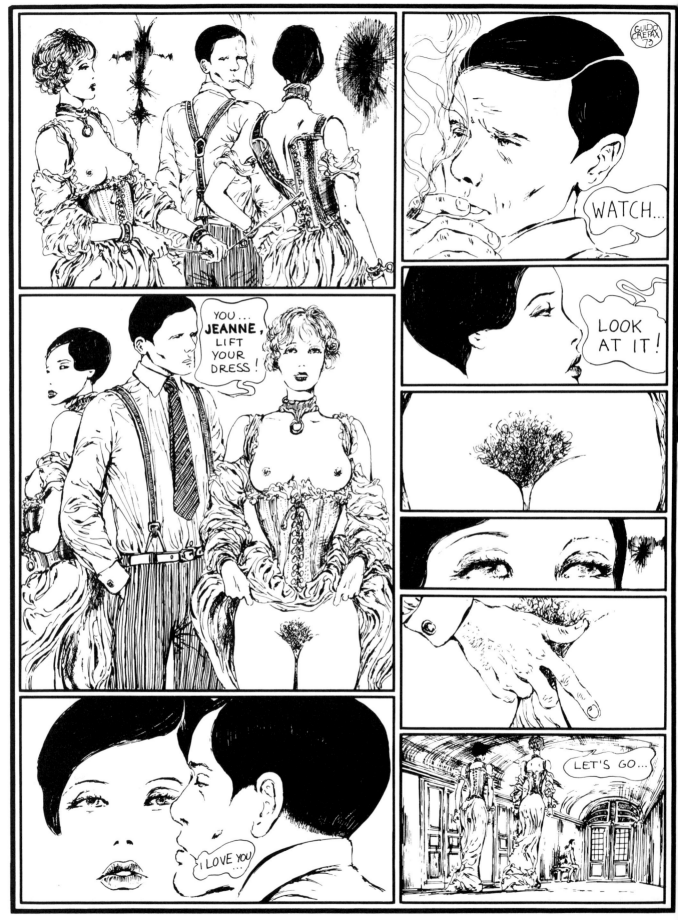

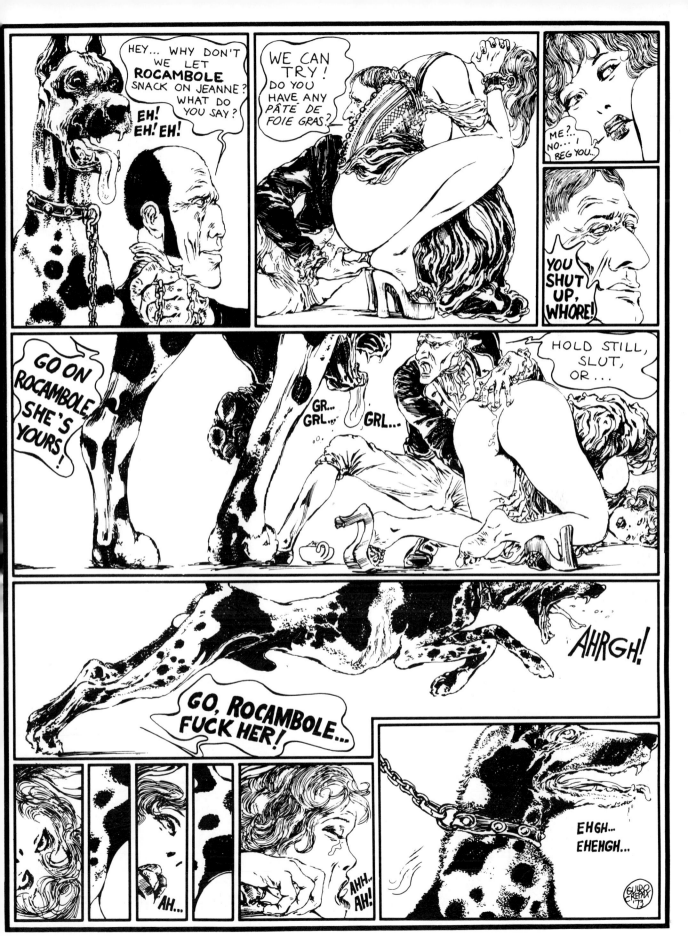

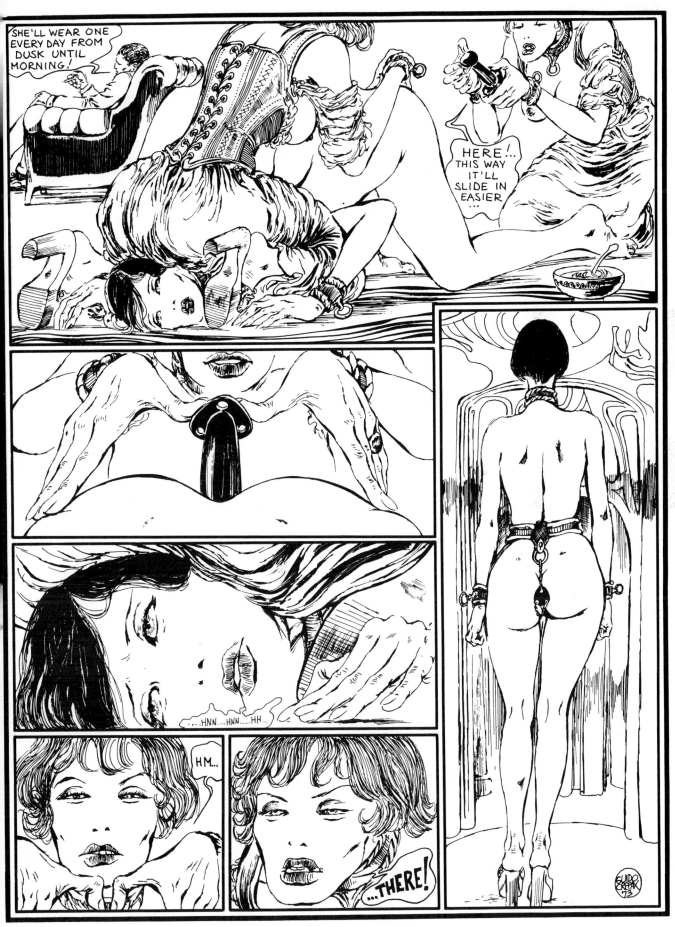

215

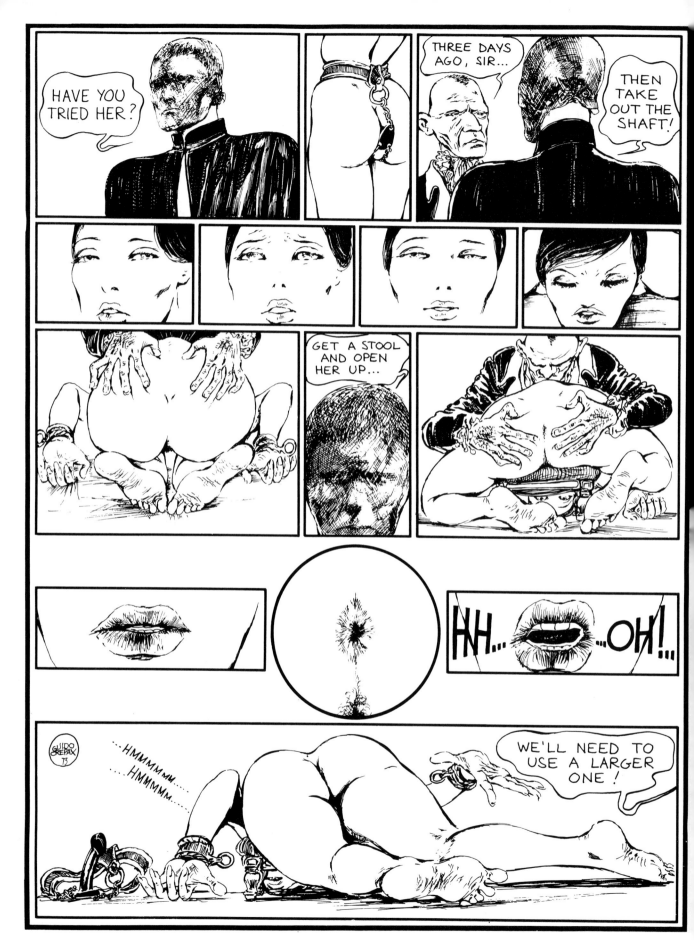

KNEEL
DOWN...

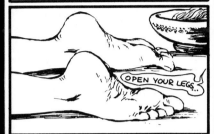

OPEN YOUR LEGS...

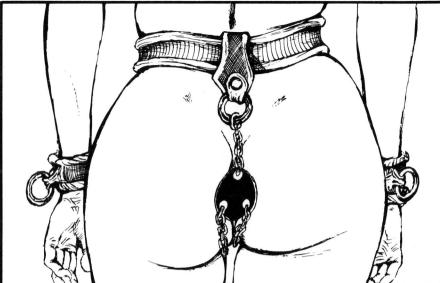

TZ!...TZ!...

WIDER!

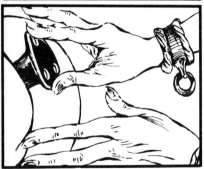

THAT'S THE
LARGEST
SIZE...

....AHHHH......

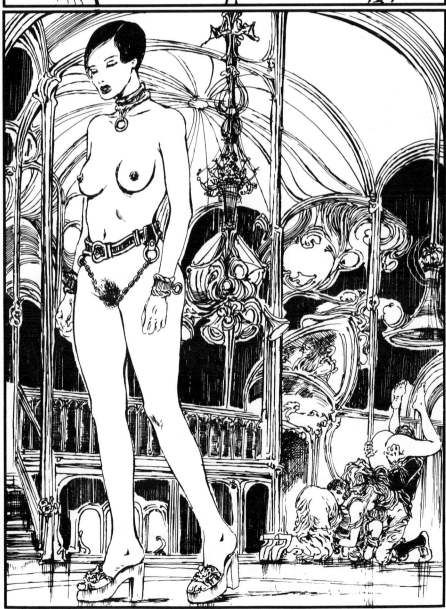

AH!

THAT'S ENOUGH, GASTON, LAY HER DOWN... THEN TURN HER OVER...

AHH!

OOH! OH OH HM OH AH!

AH... AHHH... AH... AHHH...

RESUME YOUR HOUSECLEANING ...TONIGHT YOU'LL BE FLOGGED!

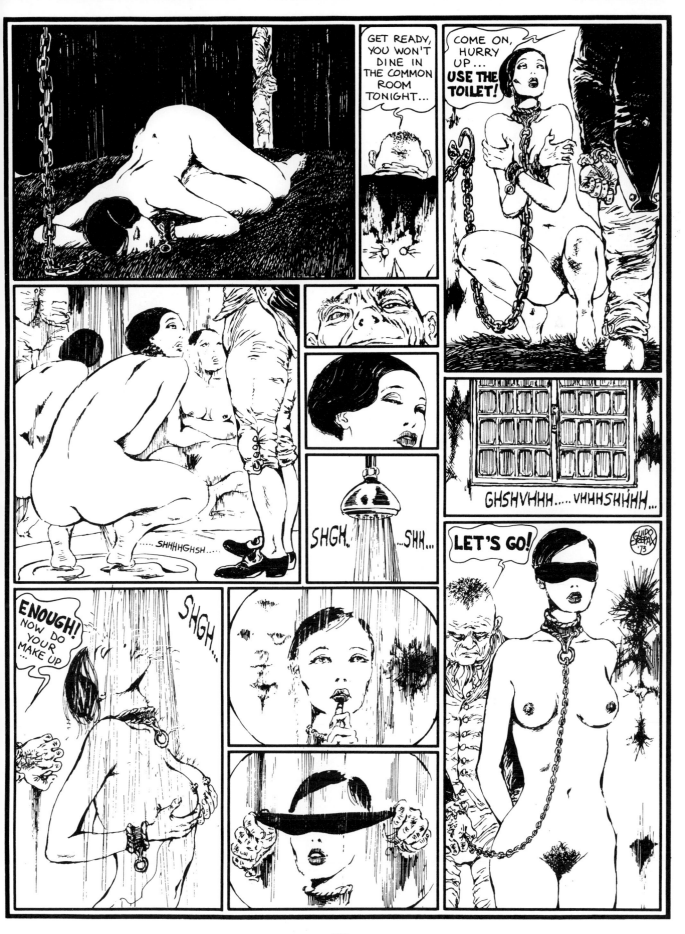

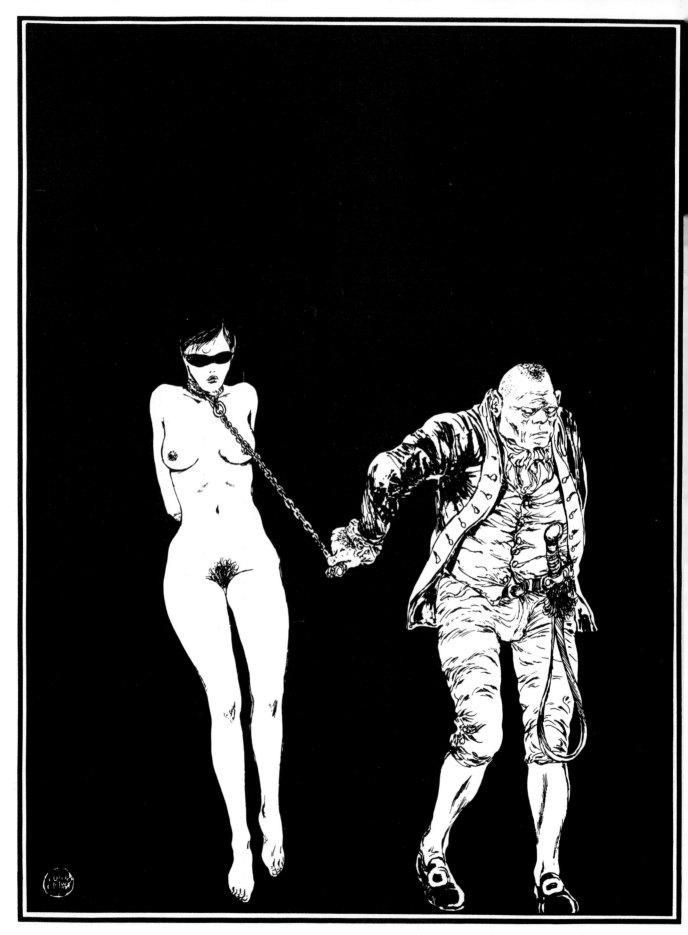

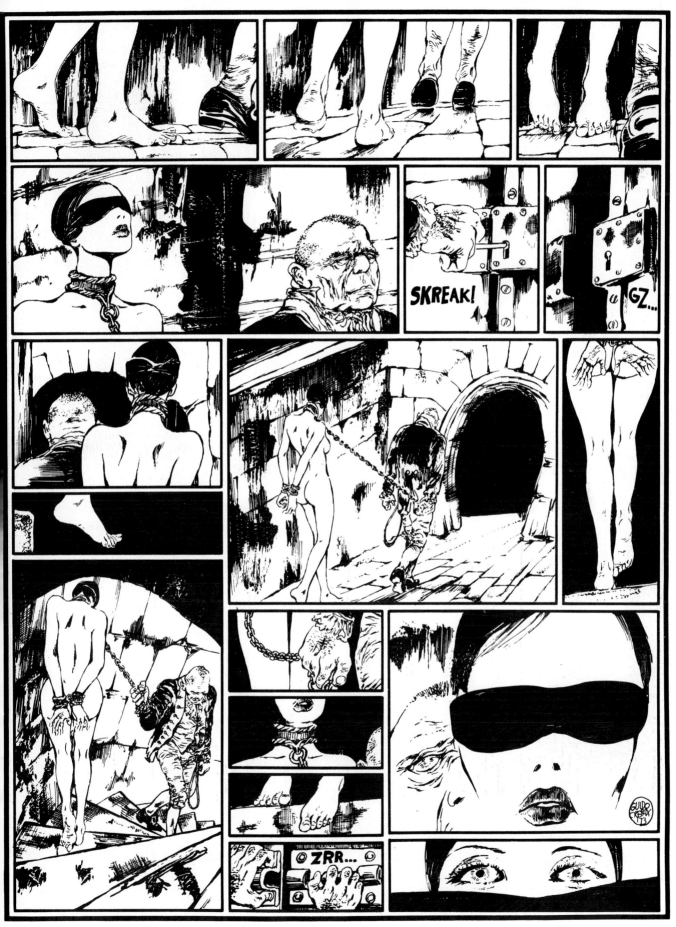

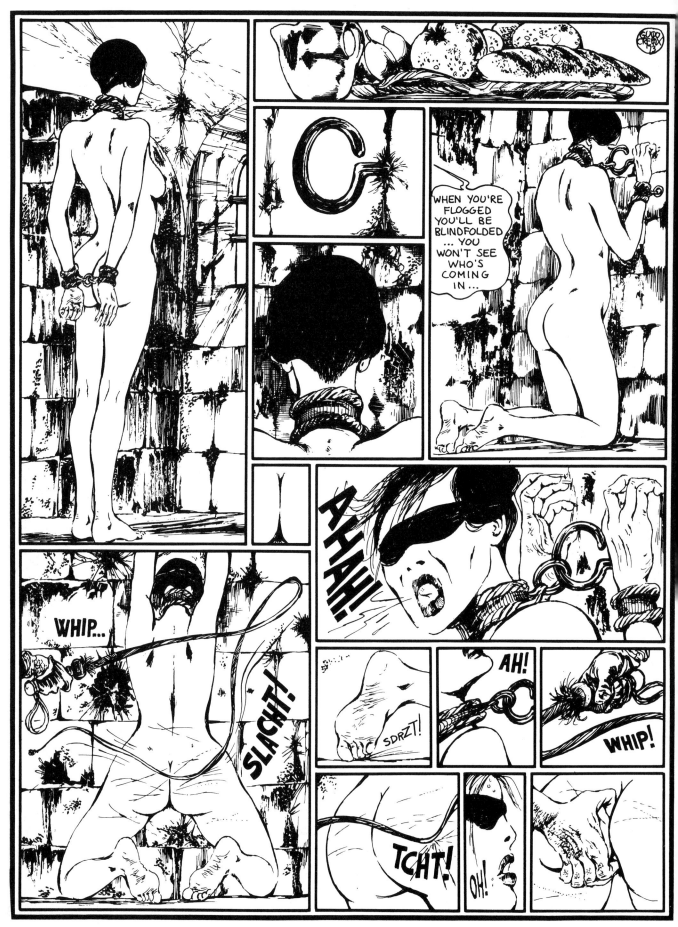

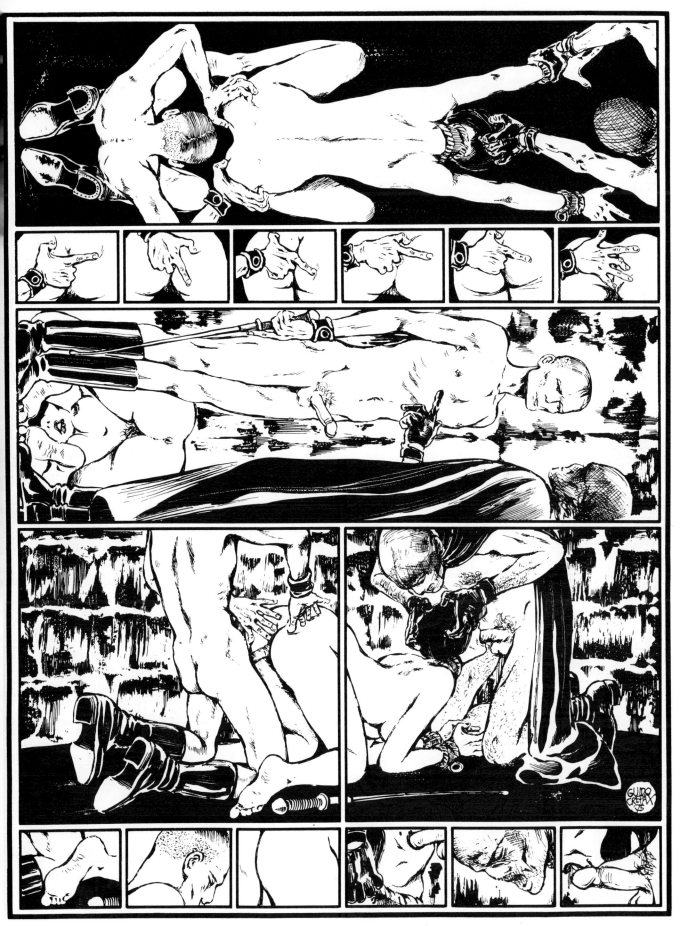

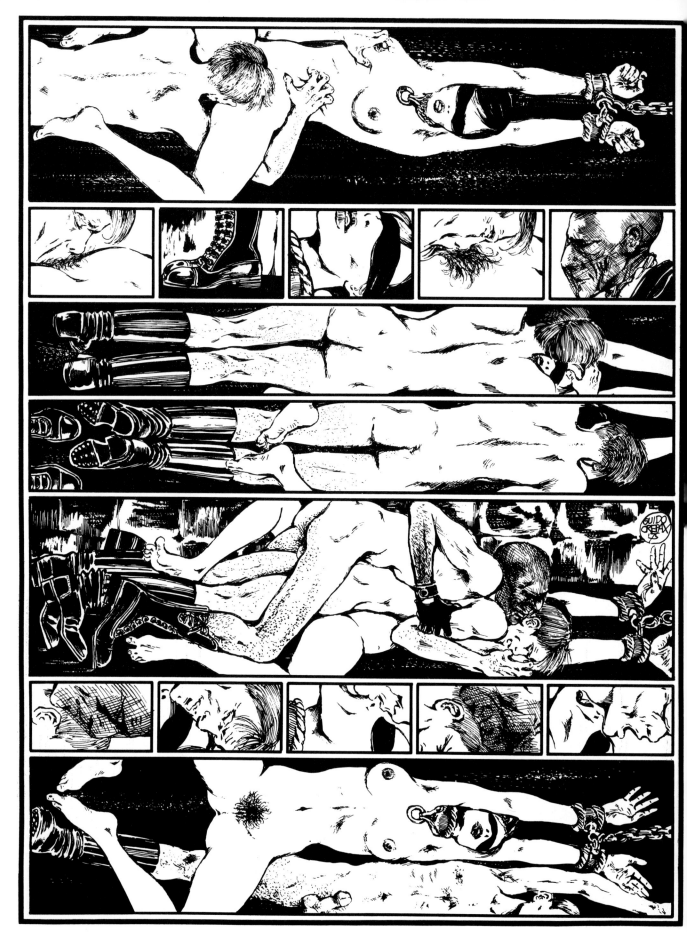

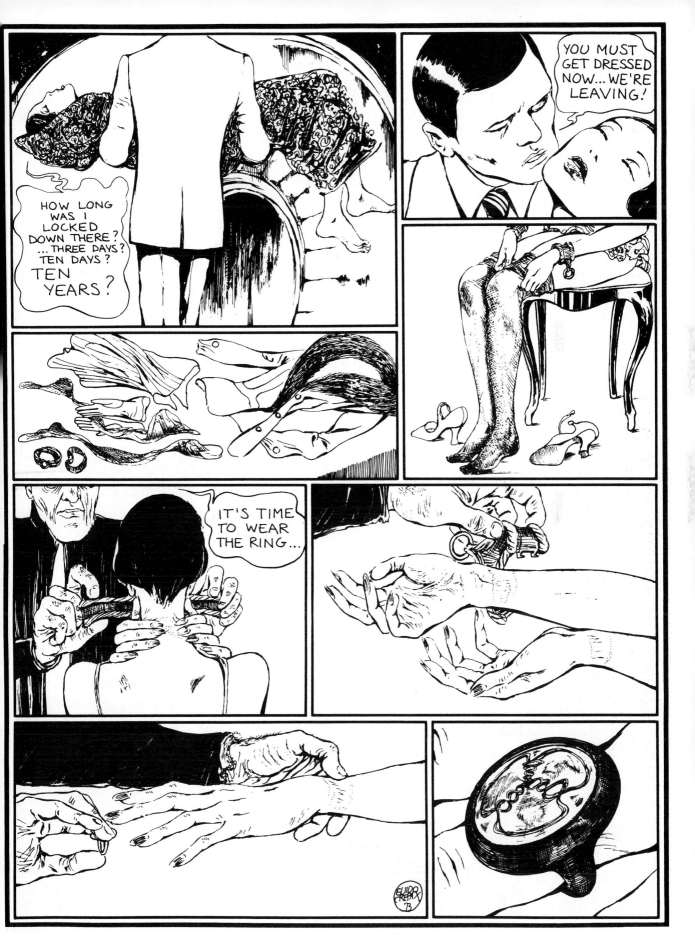

Sir Stephen

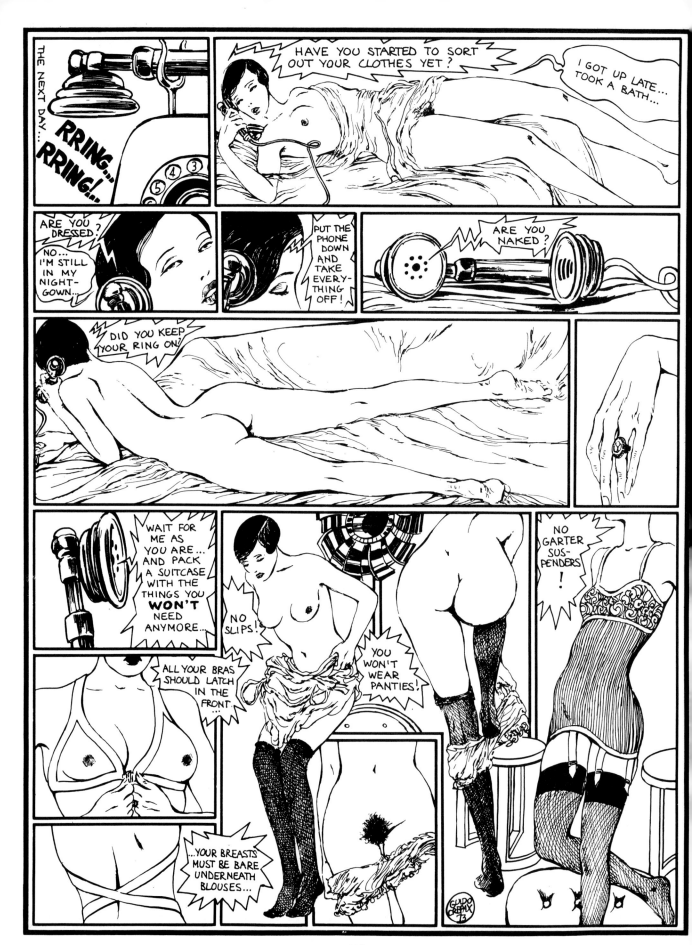

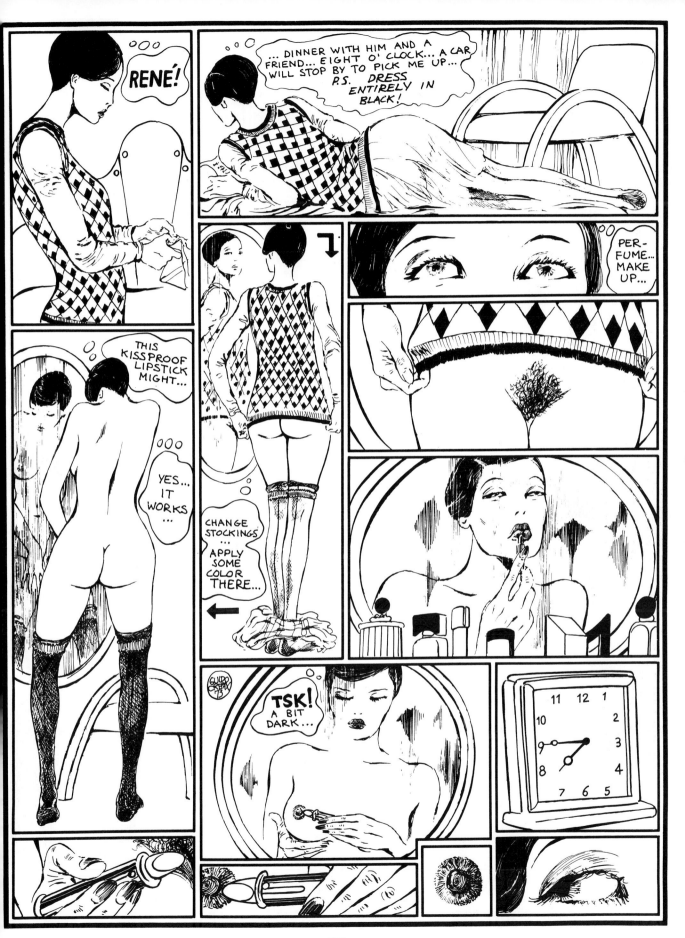

239

I DON'T BELIEVE RENÉ HAS TOLD YOU MUCH ABOUT HIS FAMILY... STILL, PERHAPS YOU'RE AWARE THAT BEFORE MARRYING HIS FATHER, HIS MOTHER WAS MARRIED TO AN ENGLISHMAN WHO ALREADY HAD A SON ...

... I AM THAT SON...

THEREFORE, IN A SENSE, RENÉ AND I ARE BROTHERS... I KNOW RENÉ LOVES YOU, AND THAT YOU'VE BEEN TO ROISSY... THE FREEDOM BETWEEN RENÉ AND I IS SO ABSOLUTE THAT WHATEVER I OWN IS ALSO HIS... AND ANYTHING THAT BELONGS TO HIM IS MINE ALSO... WOULD YOU AGREE TO BE A PART OF THIS? BEFORE YOU ANSWER KEEP IN MIND THAT I SHALL ONLY BE ANOTHER ASPECT OF YOUR LOVER, YOU WILL STILL HAVE ONLY ONE MASTER!

IF YOU GIVE YOUR CONSENT, I'LL PERSONALLY EXPLAIN TO YOU SIR STEPHEN'S PREFERENCES ...

DEMANDS!

I'M YOURS, RENÉ ...I'LL BE WHATEVER YOU WANT ME TO BE...

NO, OURS!

REPEAT AFTER ME : I BELONG TO BOTH OF YOU! I SHALL BE WHATEVER BOTH OF YOU WANT ME TO BE!

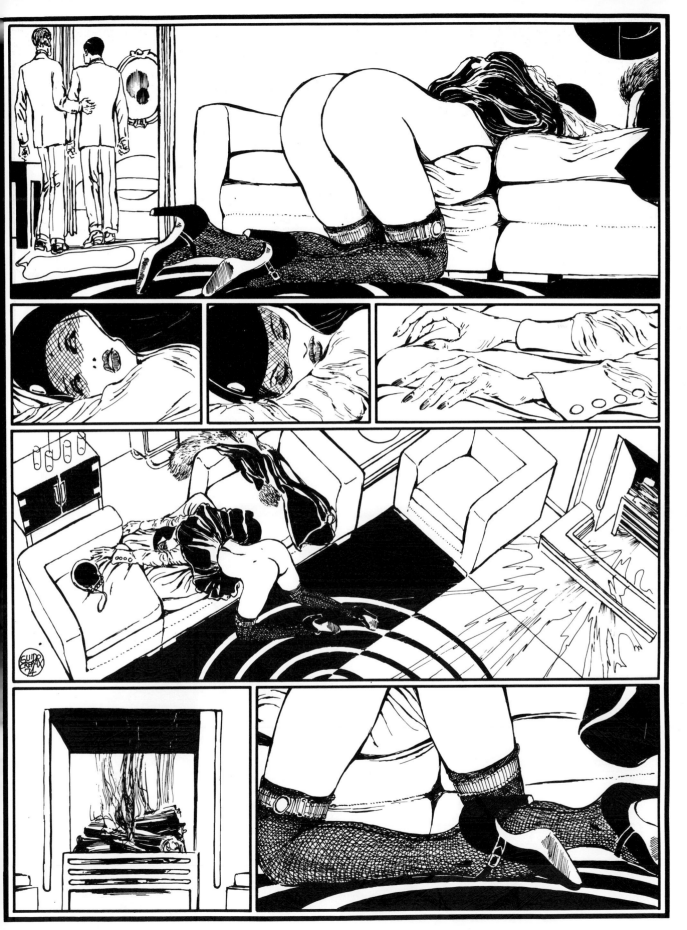

250

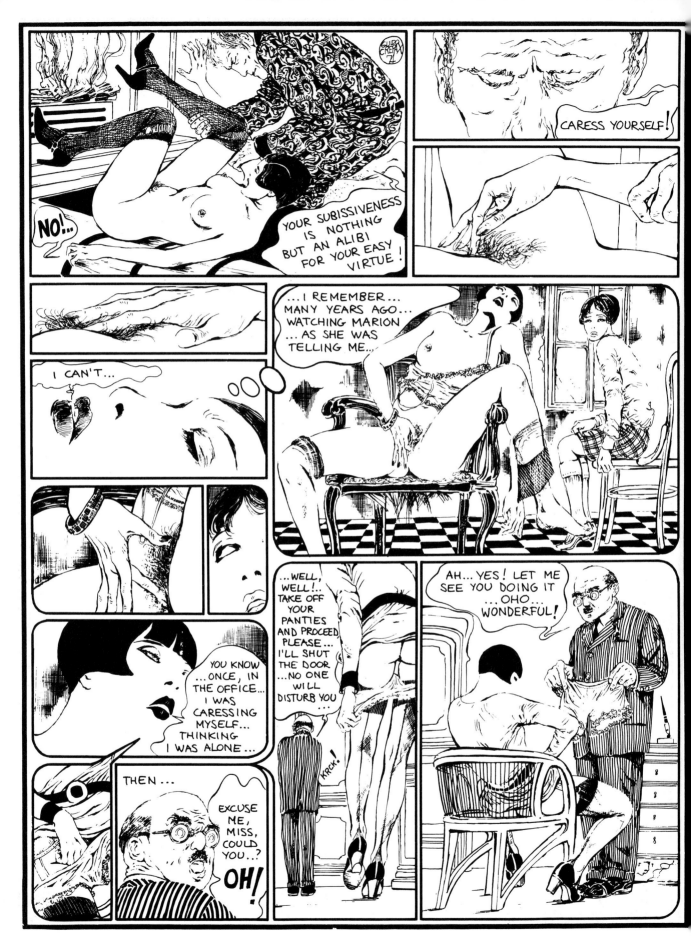

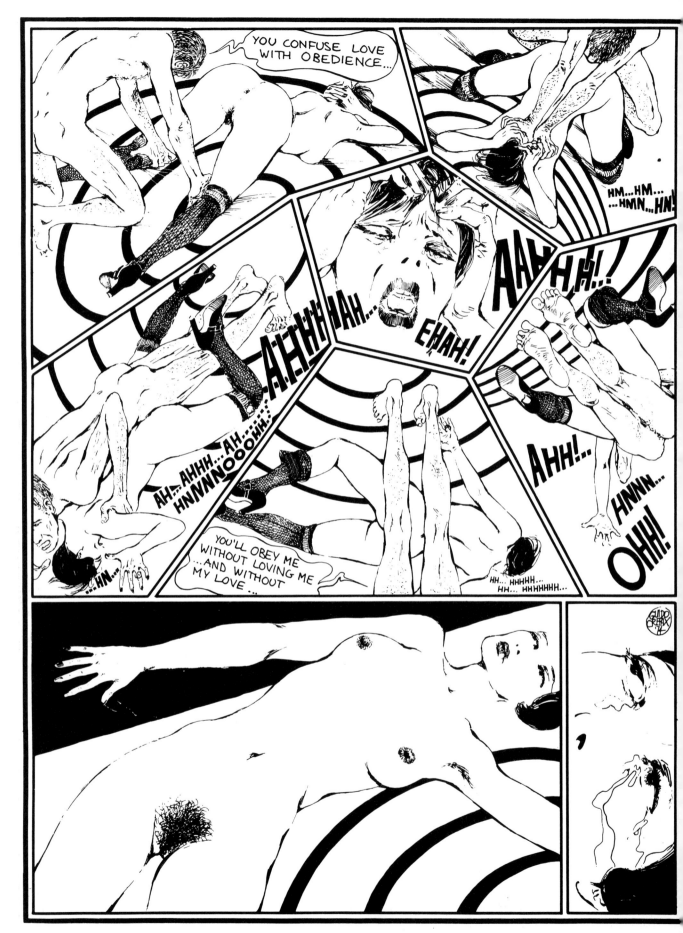

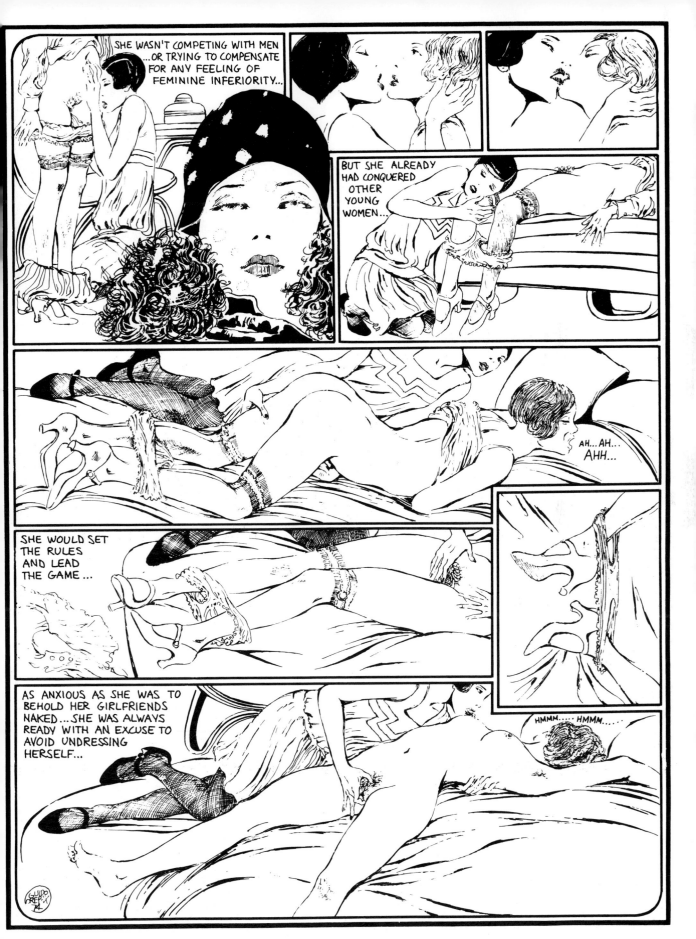

SHE WASN'T COMPETING WITH MEN ...OR TRYING TO COMPENSATE FOR ANY FEELING OF FEMININE INFERIORITY...

BUT SHE ALREADY HAD CONQUERED OTHER YOUNG WOMEN...

AH...AH... AHH...

SHE WOULD SET THE RULES AND LEAD THE GAME...

AS ANXIOUS AS SHE WAS TO BEHOLD HER GIRLFRIENDS NAKED...SHE WAS ALWAYS READY WITH AN EXCUSE TO AVOID UNDRESSING HERSELF...

HMMM......HMMM......

SINCE SHE FIRST HAD FEMALE LOVERS,
SHE NEVER ALLOWED THEM
TO RETURN HER CARESSES...

COME SPRING SHE THOUGHT
SHE HAD FINALLY FOUND
THE COURAGE TO FACE
JACQUELINE...

ARE THEY
FOR ME?

259

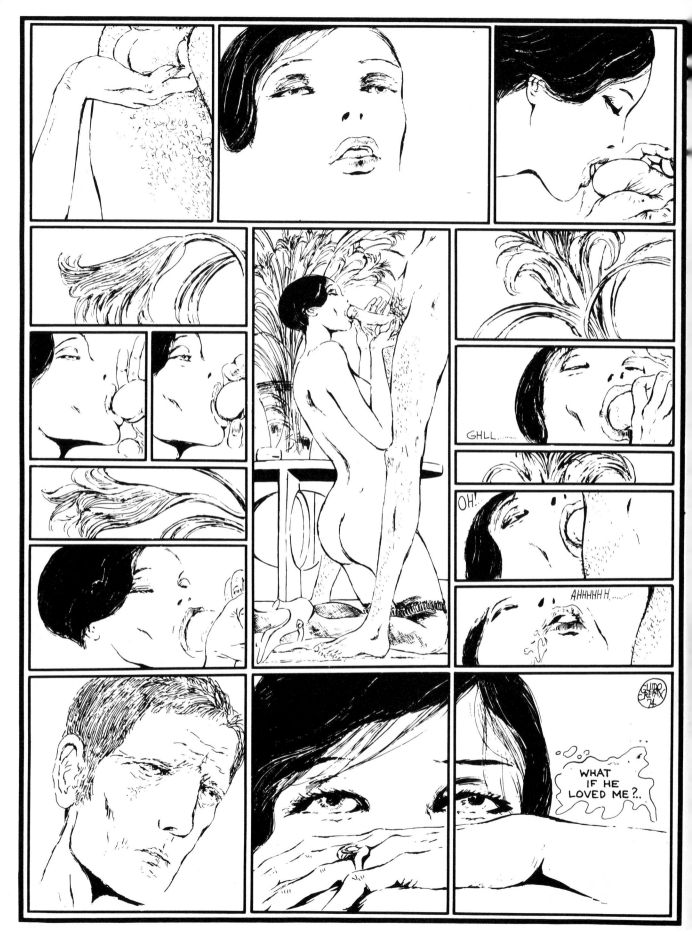

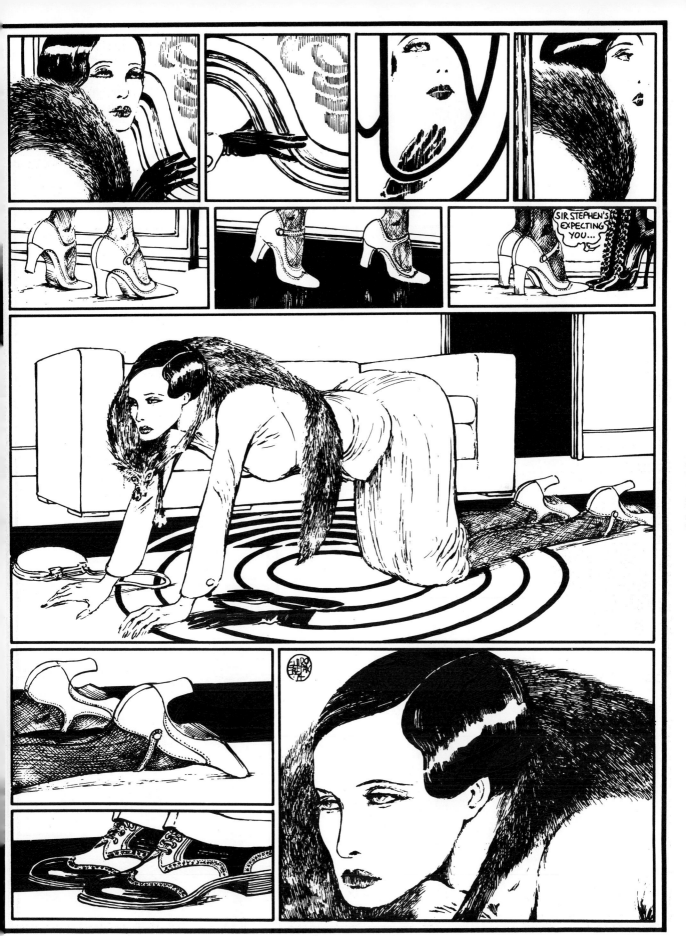

263

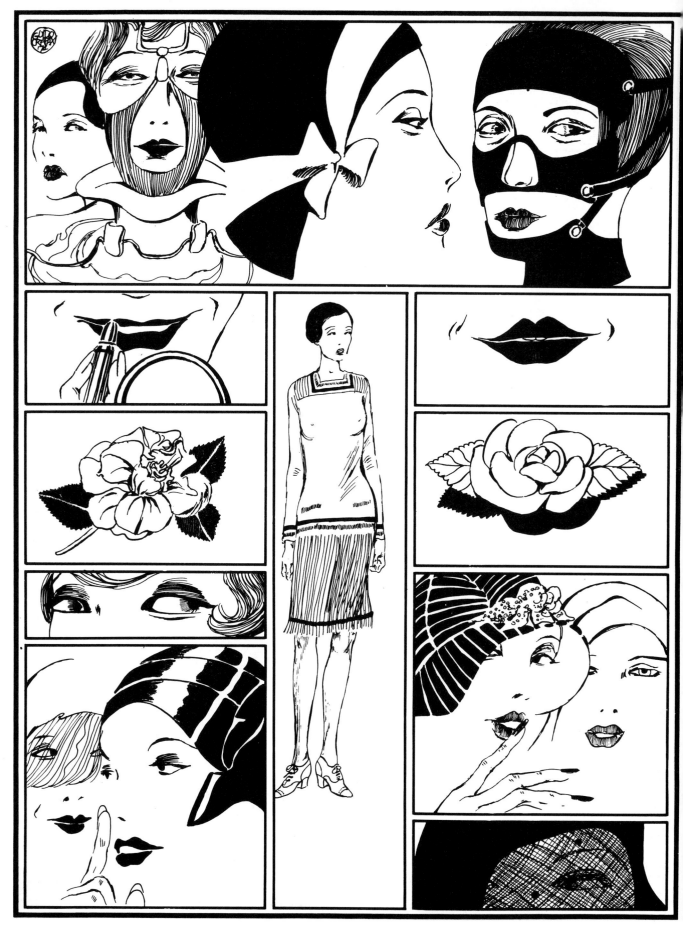

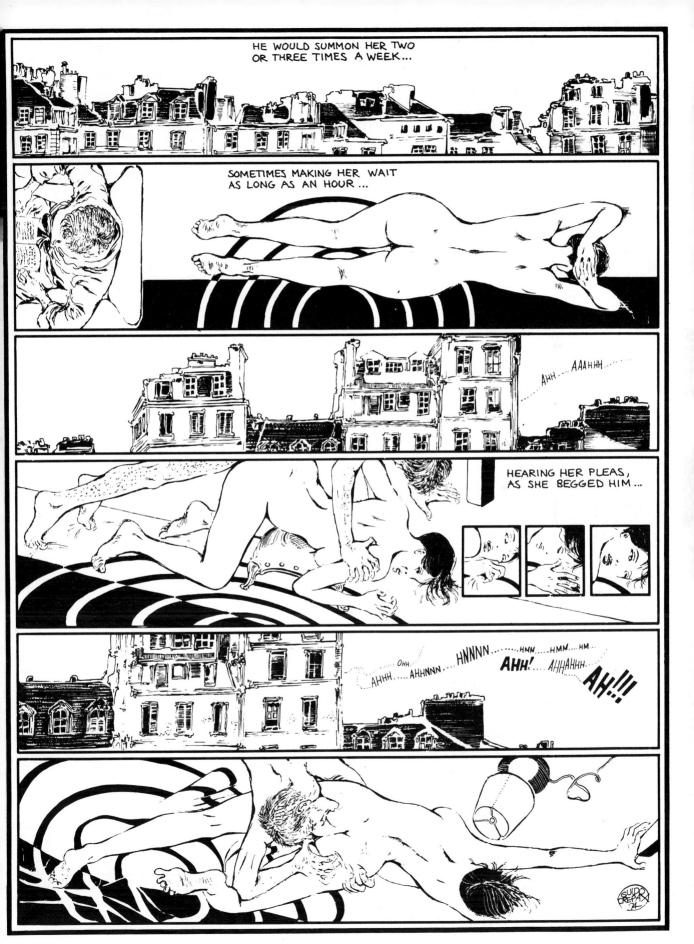

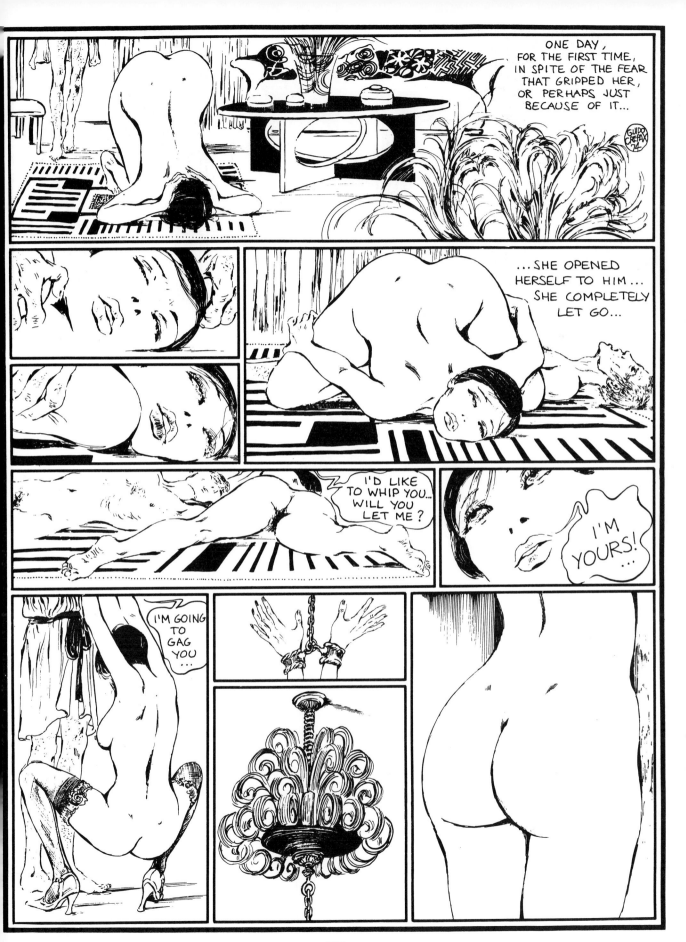

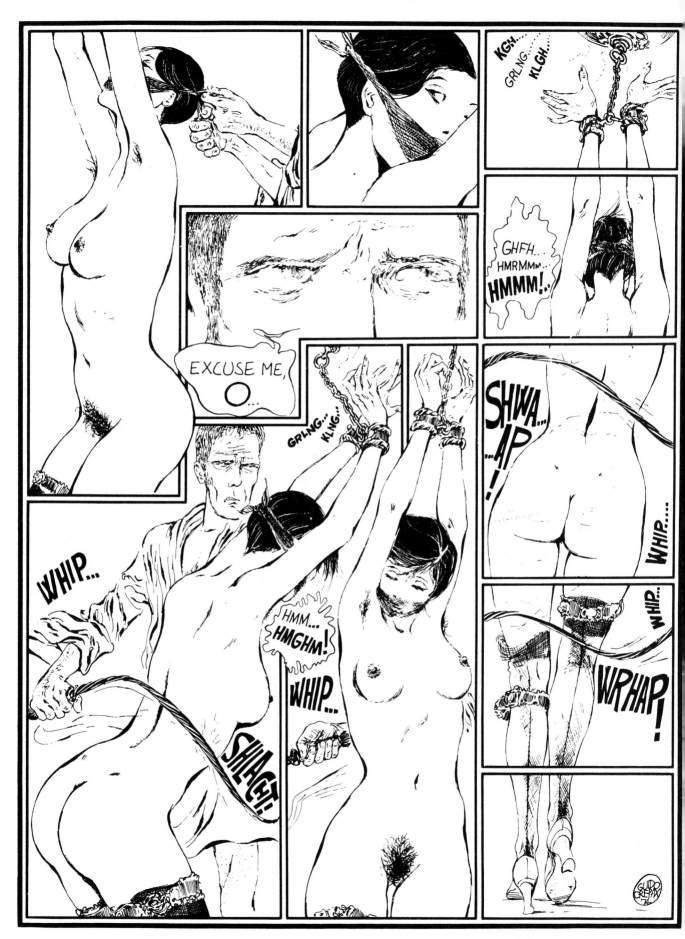

THAT EVENING SHE WOULD HAVE LIKED TO GO WITH RENE TO A PARTY...

YOU COULD TELL HIM I'LL GO OVER TOMORROW... GIVE HIM SOME PRETEXT... PLEASE... PLEASE, DARLING!

SHE WANTED TO DISOBEY... SHE NEEDS A GOOD PUNISHMENT...

FINE!

RENE' WENT BY HIMSELF...

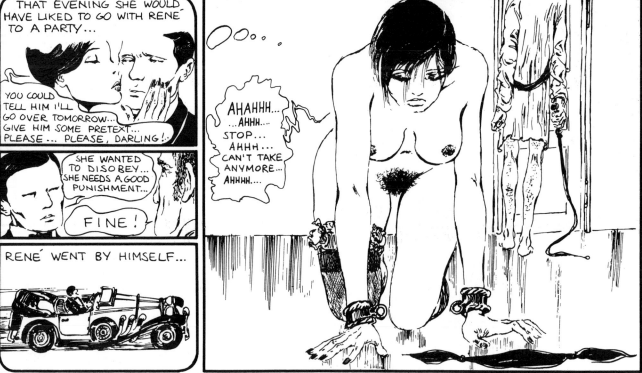

AHAHHH...
...AHHH...
STOP...
AHHH...
CAN'T TAKE
ANYMORE...
AHHHH....

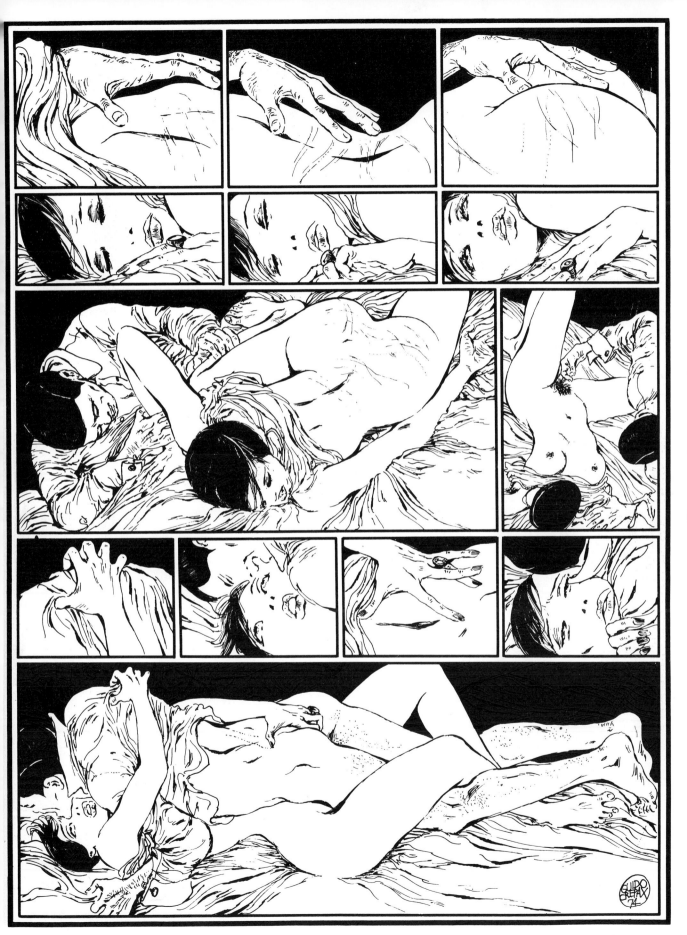

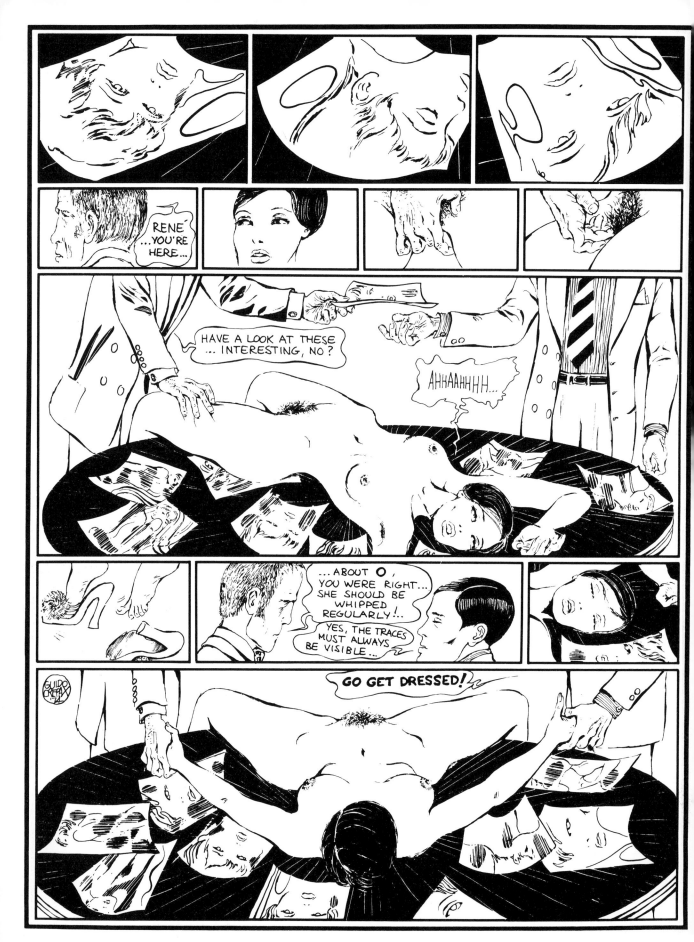

Anne-Marie & The Rings

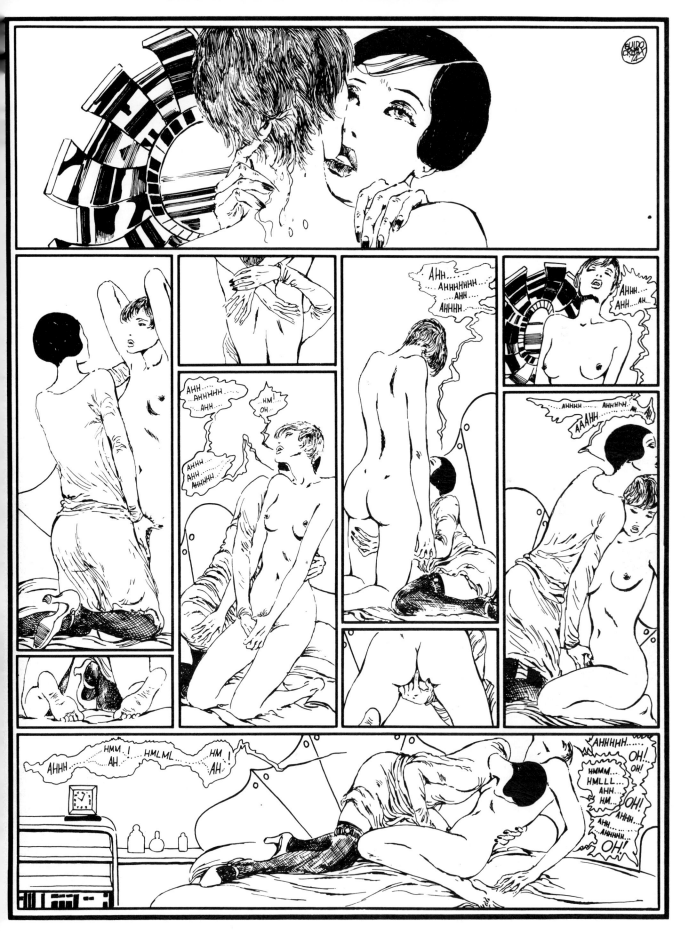

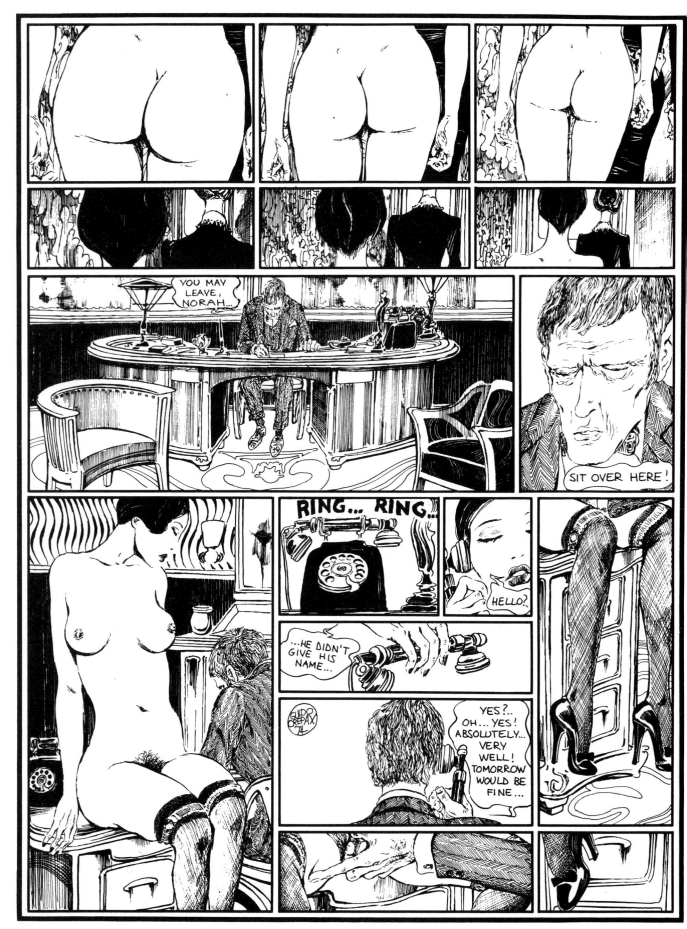

OHHH...

RENE'S IN LONDON...WE'RE GOING TO ANNE-MARIE'S...DON'T BOTHER PACKING A SUITCASE... YOU WON'T NEED ANYTHING!

HERE'S O... YOU KNOW WHAT HAS TO BE DONE...WHEN WILL SHE BE READY?

YOU HAVEN'T TOLD HER? ALL RIGHT...I'LL BEGIN IMMEDIATELY! ALLOW FOR ABOUT TEN DAYS...

HEH.. HEH.. HEH

I IMAGINE YOU'LL WANT TO PUT THE RINGS AND MONOGRAM ON YOURSELF? ... YOU, O, GO INSIDE AND TAKE OFF YOUR DRESS...

KNEEL DOWN IN FRONT OF SIR STEPHEN!

HEH HEH

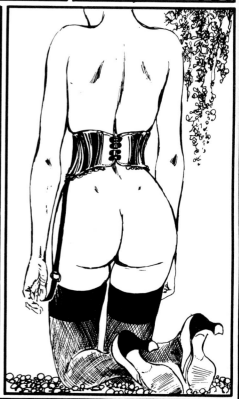

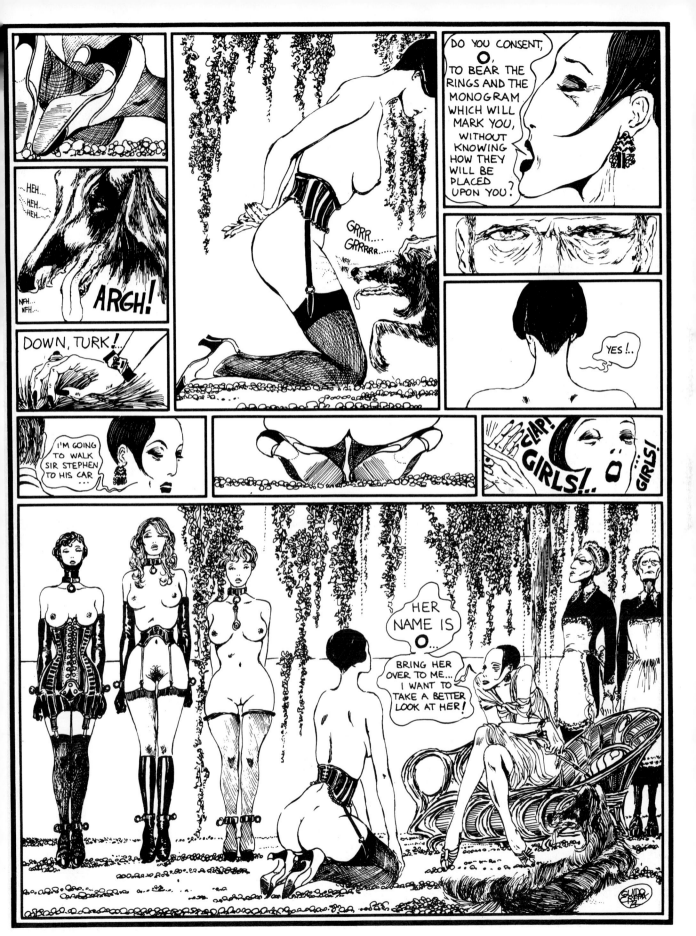

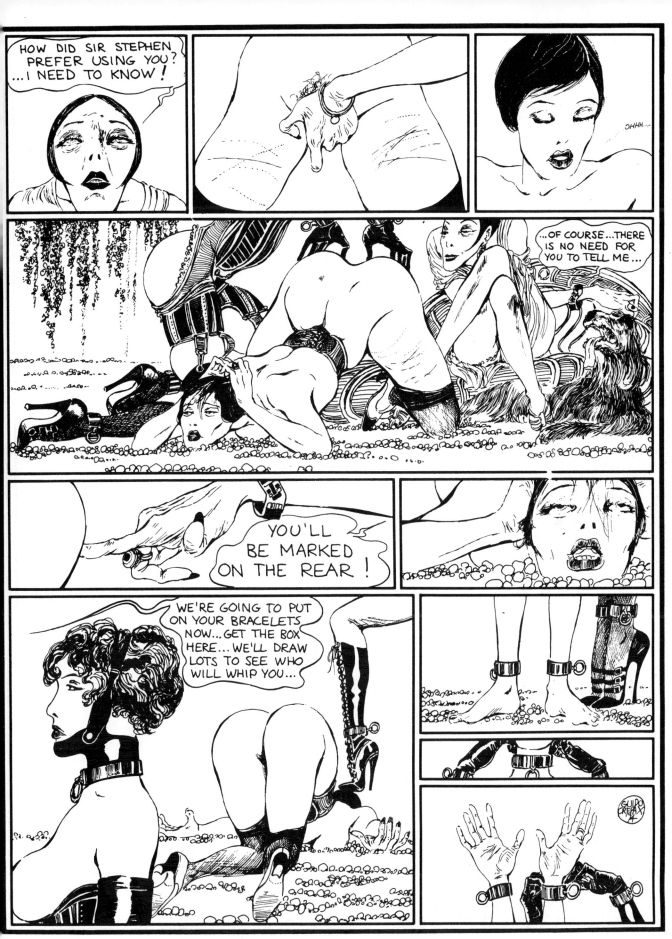

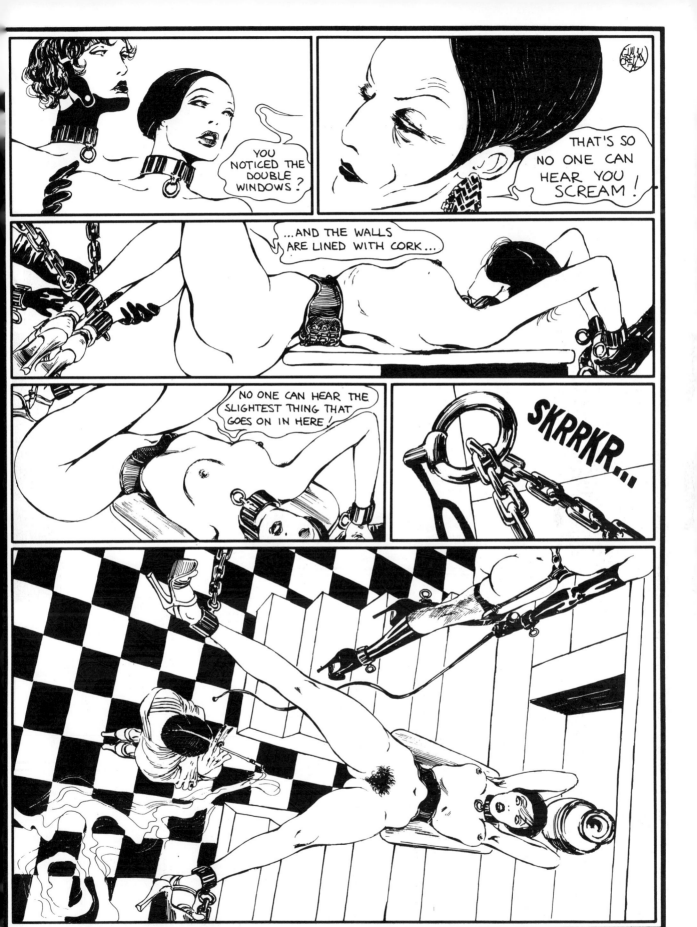

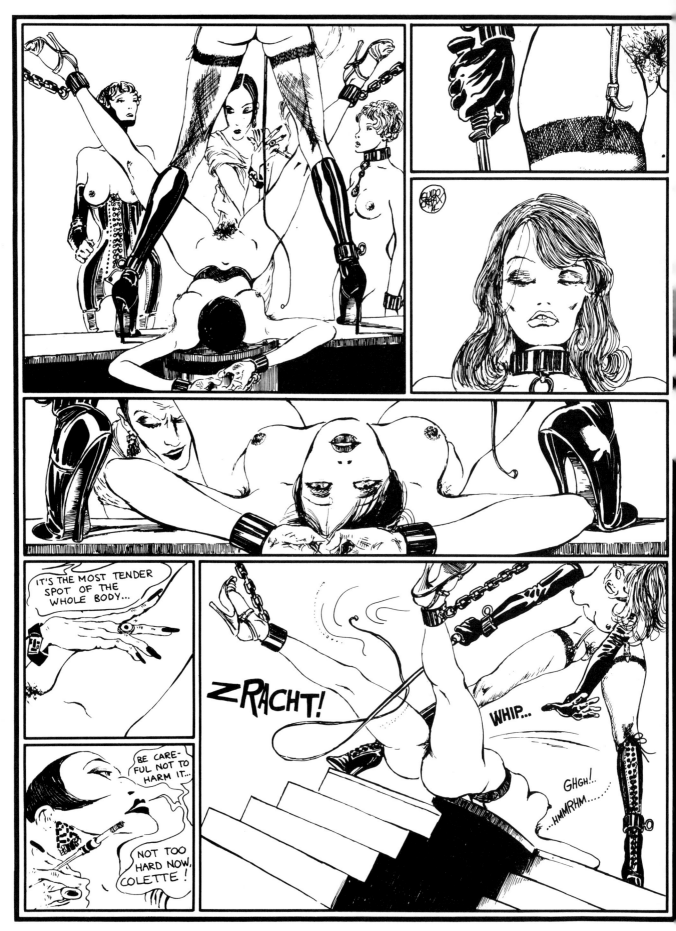

GOOD MORNING, GIRLS... FOLLOW ME... I MUST SHOW YOU SOMETHING...

HASN'T YVONNE SAID ANYTHING TO YOU ABOUT THIS? I KNOW SIR STEPHEN DIDN'T... ANYWAY... HERE ARE THE RINGS!

...THE RINGS HE WANTS YOU TO WEAR...

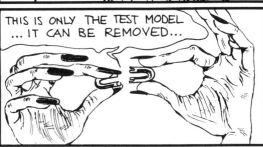

THIS IS ONLY THE TEST MODEL ...IT CAN BE REMOVED...

THE PERMANENT MODEL HAS A SPRING INSIDE, AND ONCE IT'S LOCKED IT CANNOT BE REMOVED...EXCEPT BY FILING!

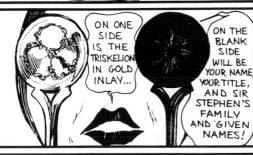

ON ONE SIDE IS THE TRISKELION IN GOLD INLAY...

ON THE BLANK SIDE WILL BE YOUR NAME, YOUR TITLE, AND SIR STEPHEN'S FAMILY AND GIVEN NAMES!

YVONNE WEARS HERS ON HER NECKLACE!

BUT YOURS WILL BE WORN ON YOUR LOINS!

LOOK...

SHOW YOURS, YVONNE, OPEN UP...

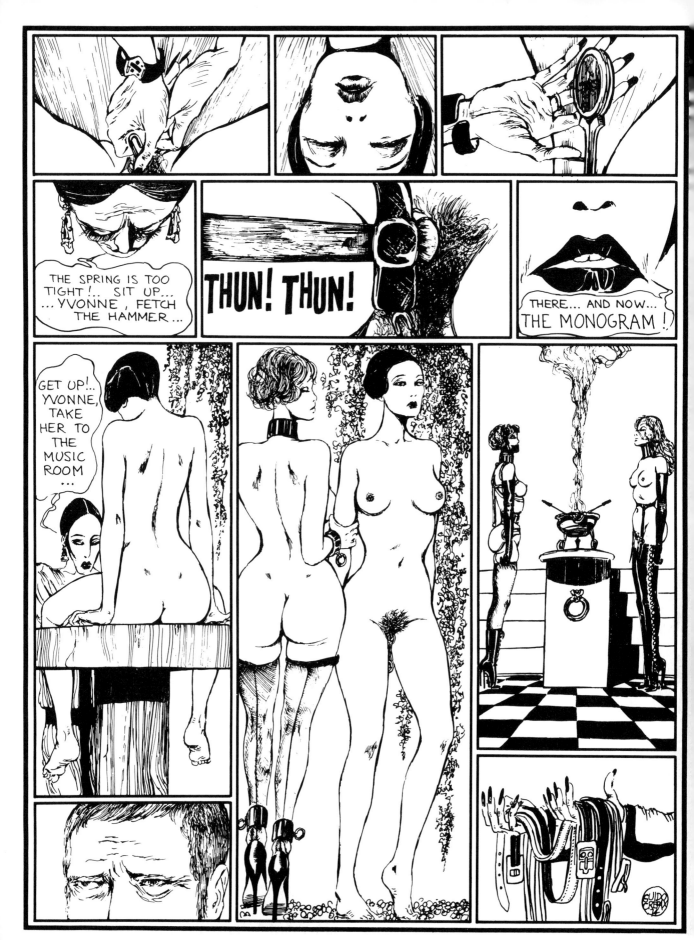

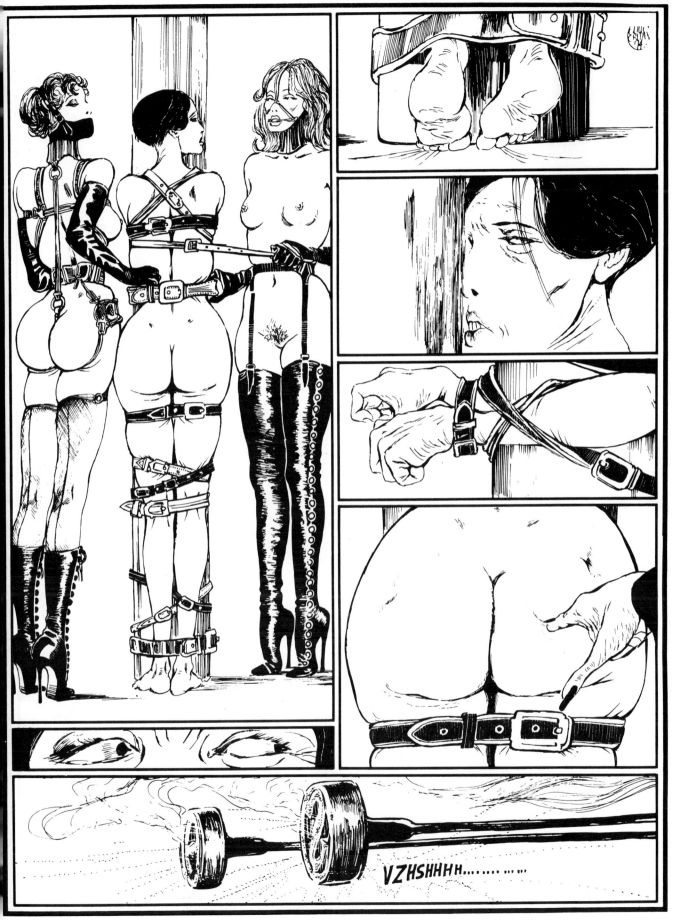

VZHSHHHH..........

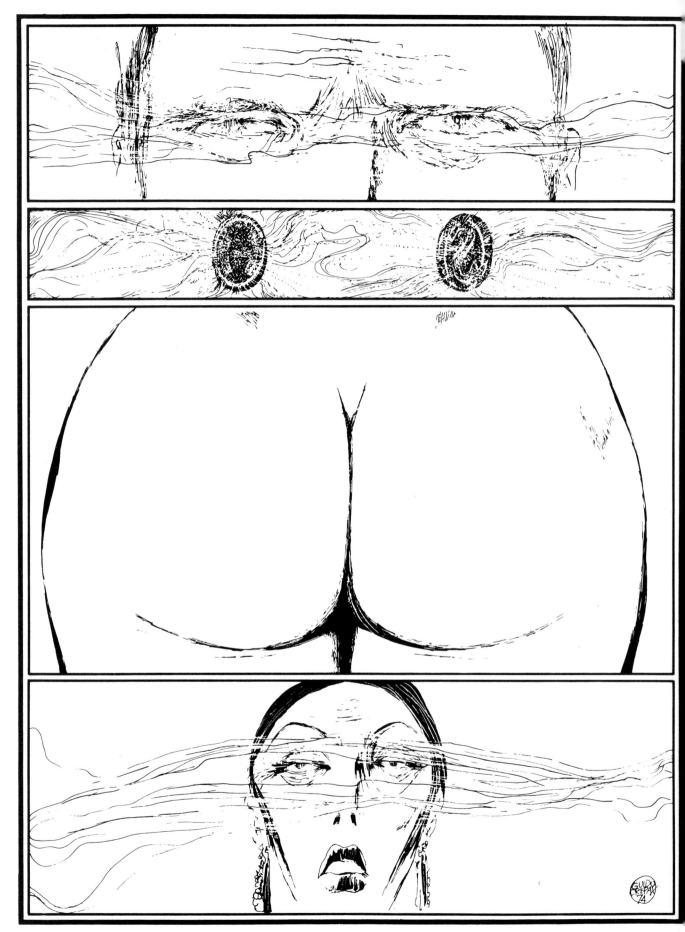

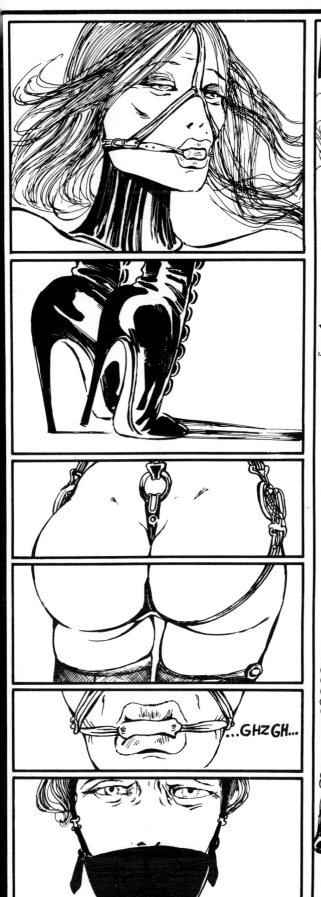

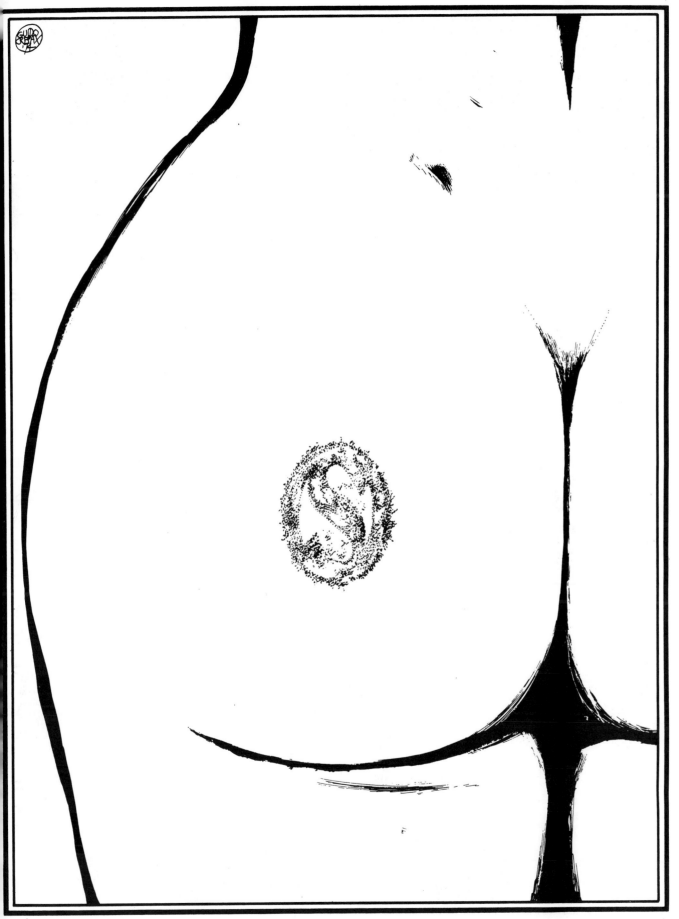

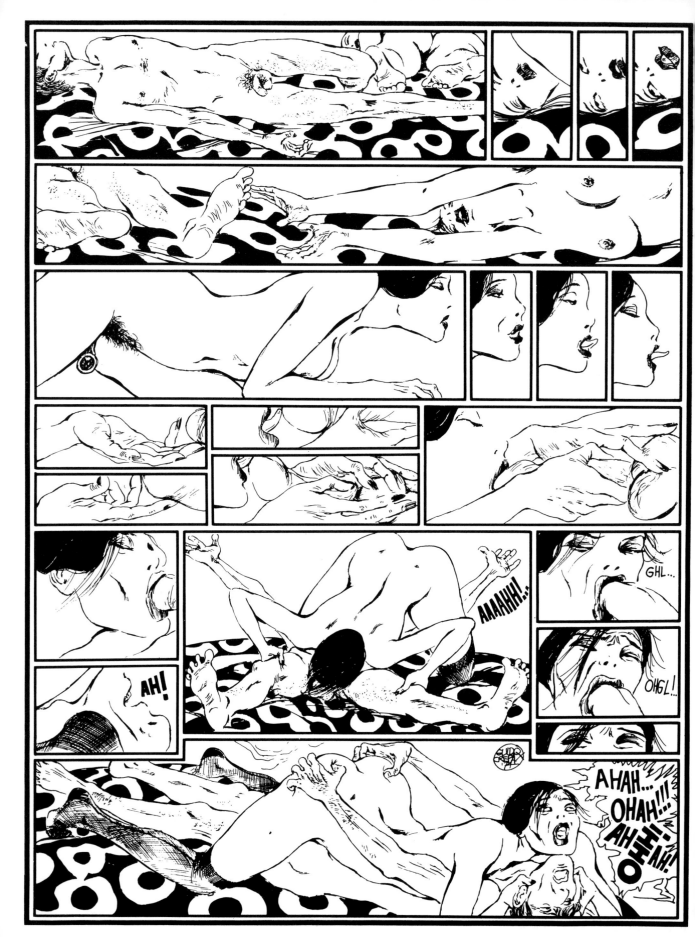

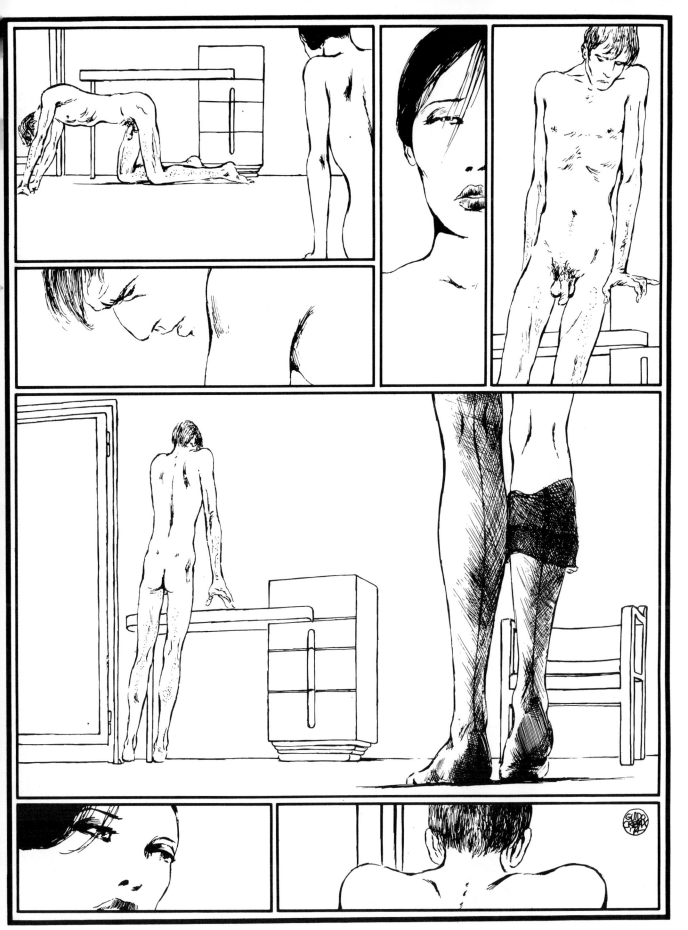

The Owl

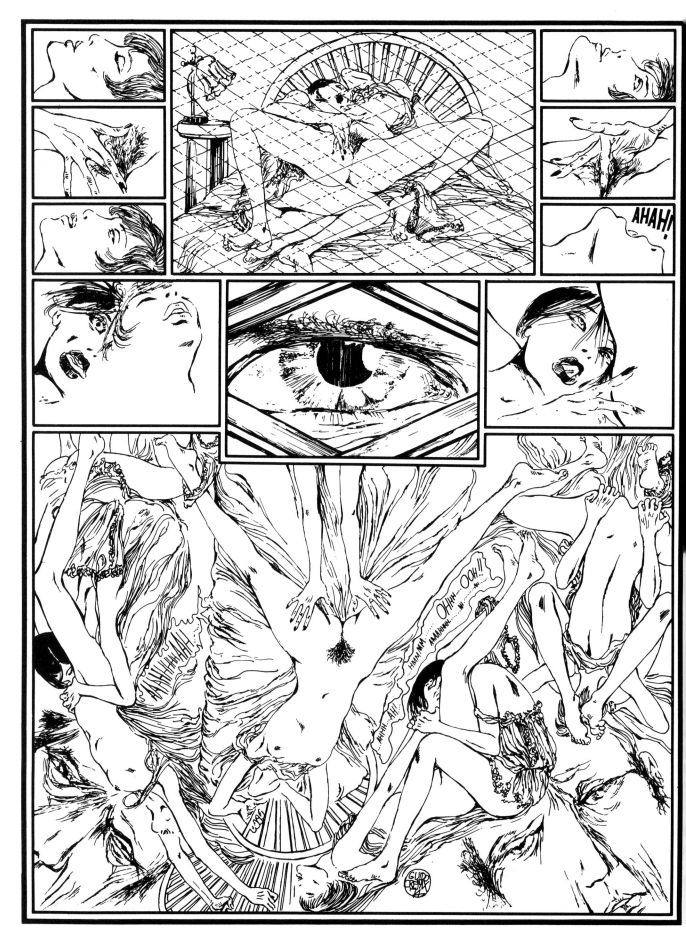

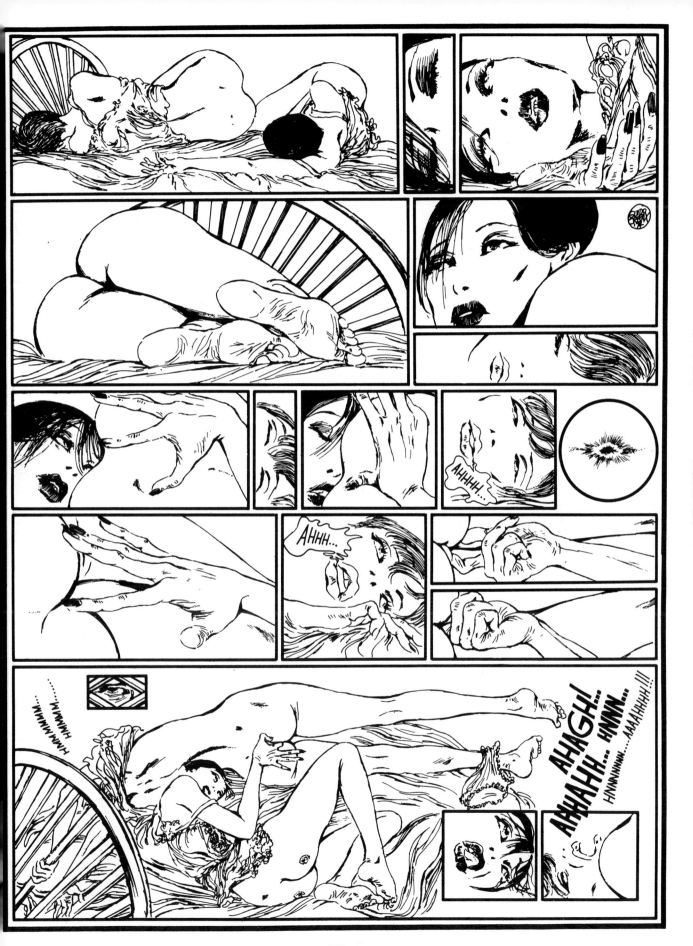

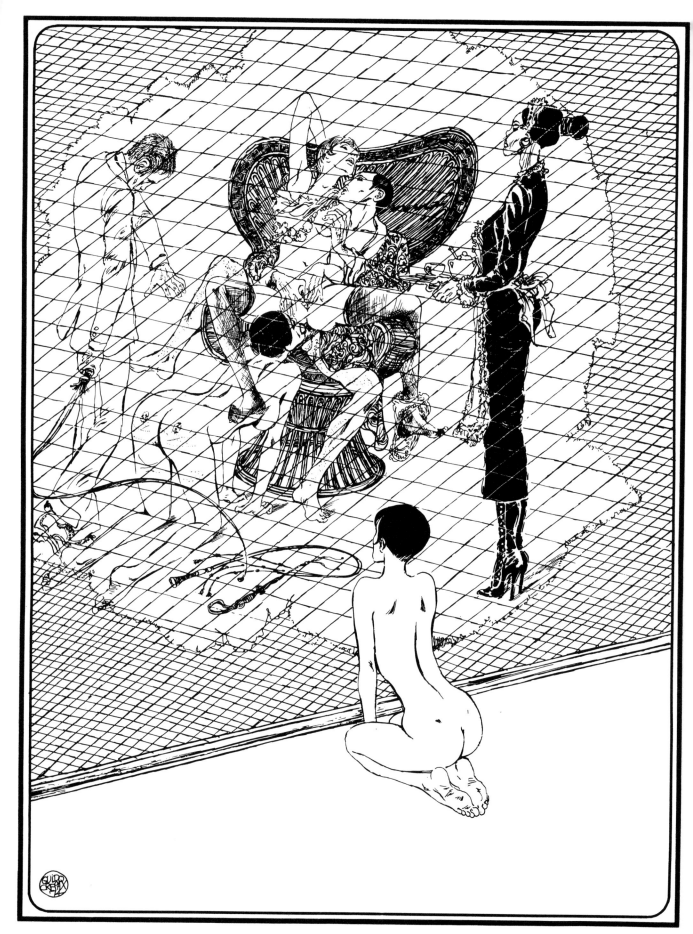

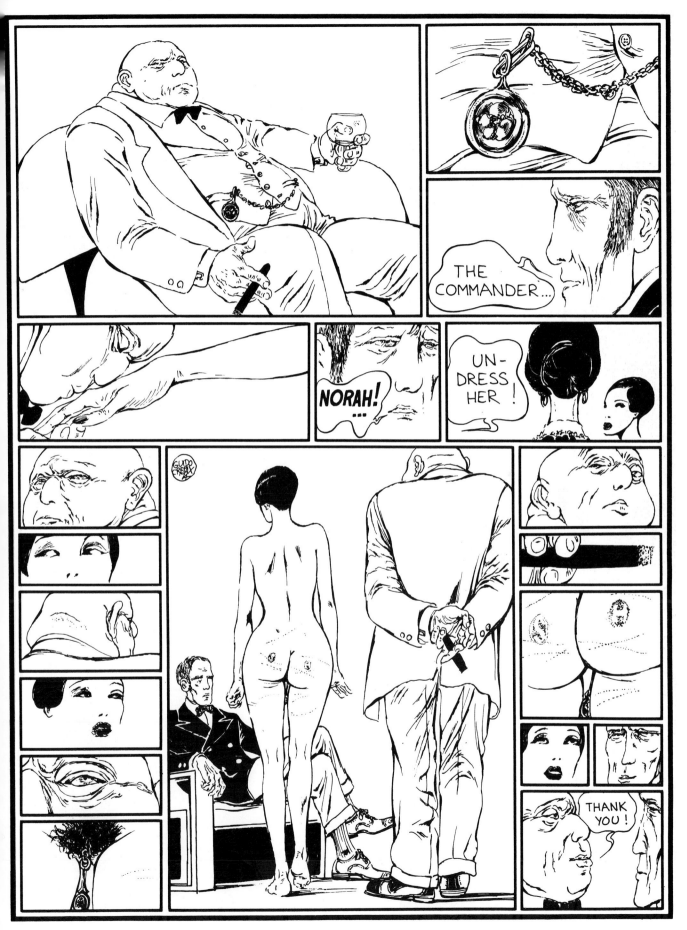

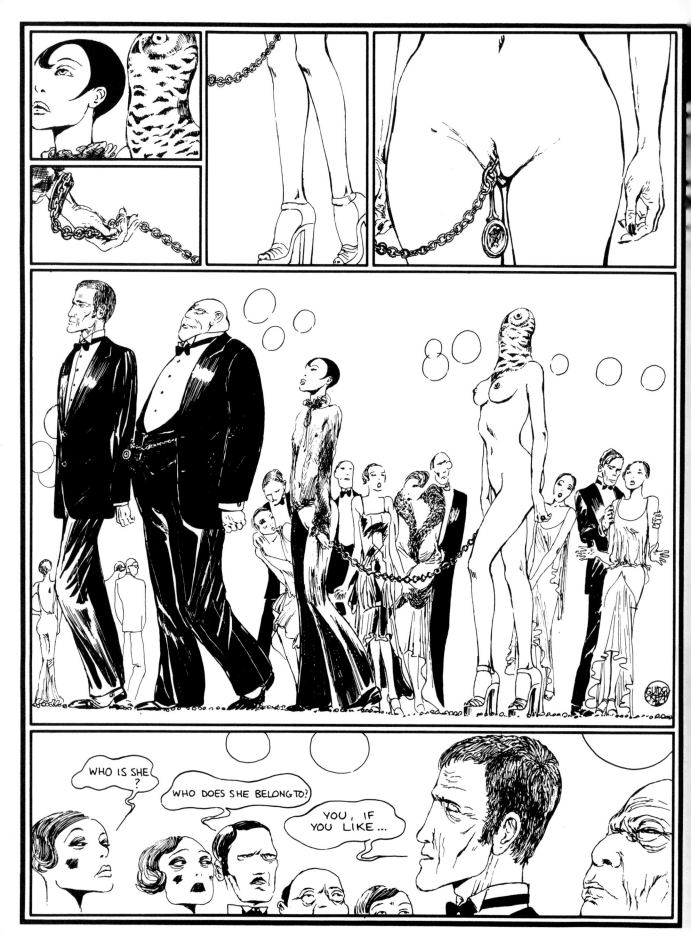

The Penthouse

STOP

NOW WE HAVE MORE TIME!...

FLASH

LET'S GO UP!

355

The Pembrokes

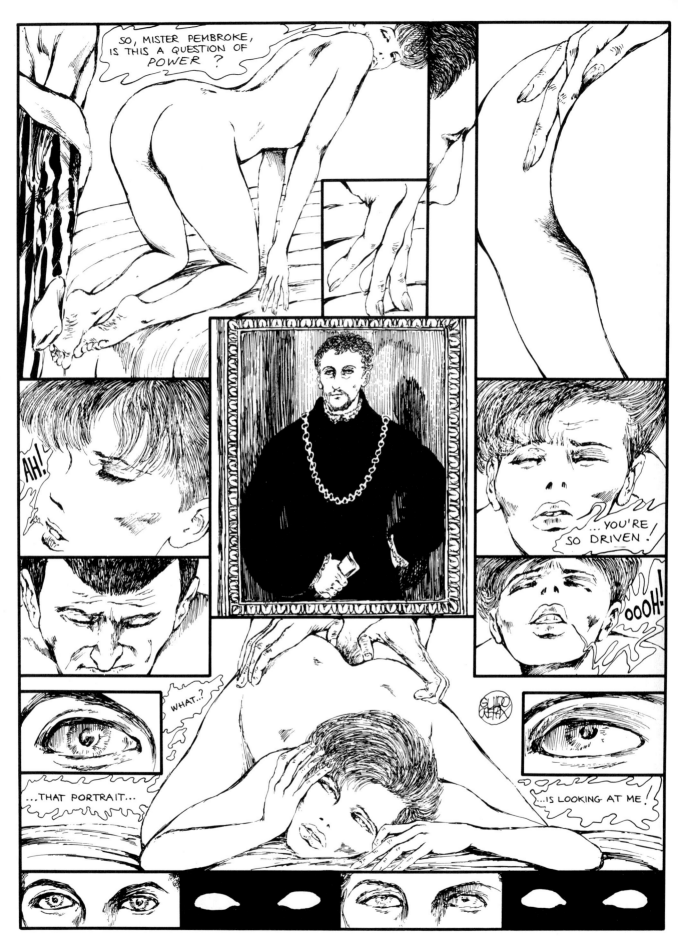

362

Madame O

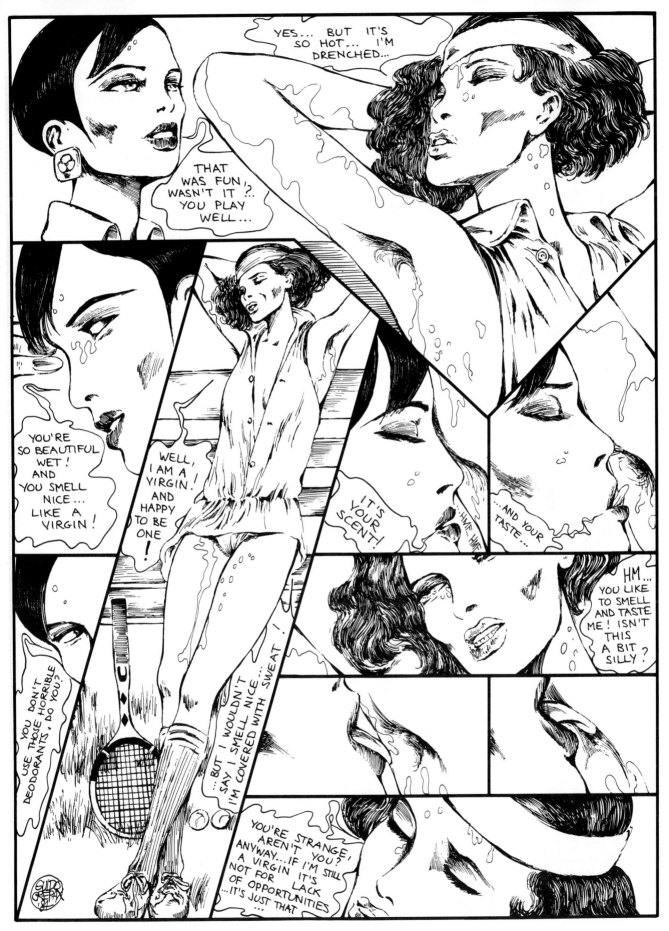

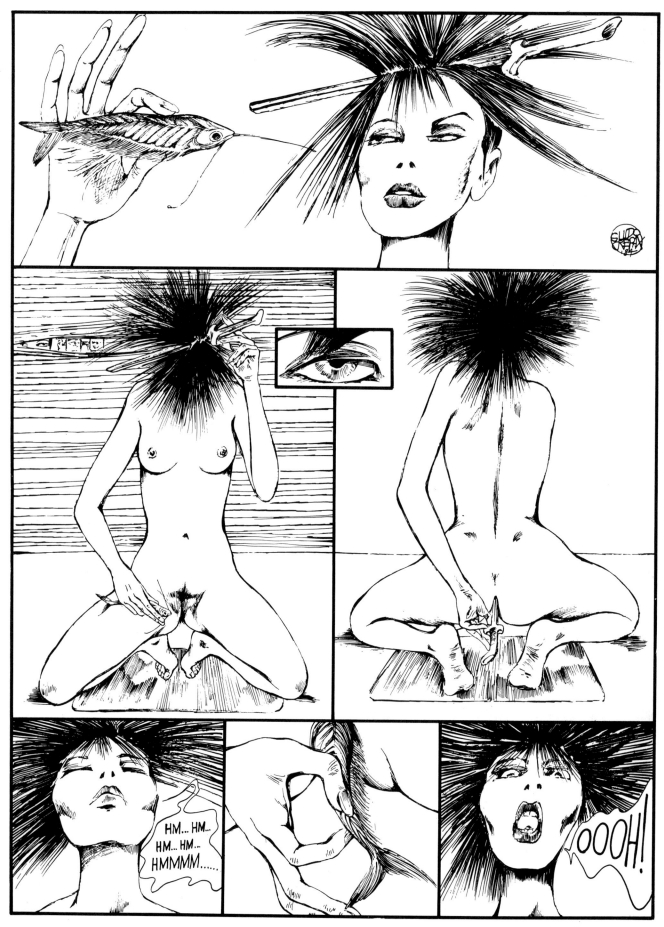

New Roissy

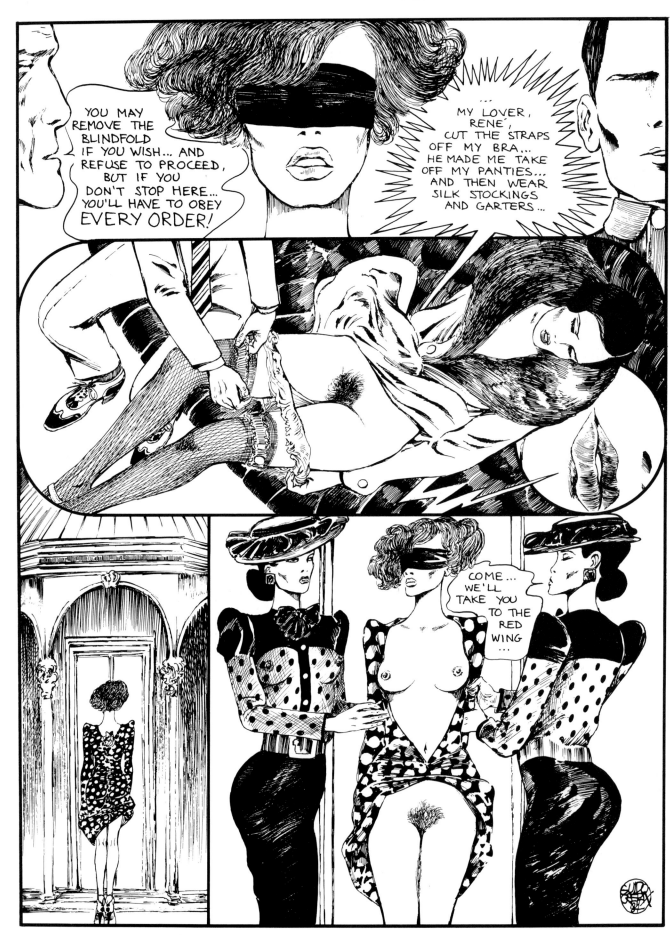

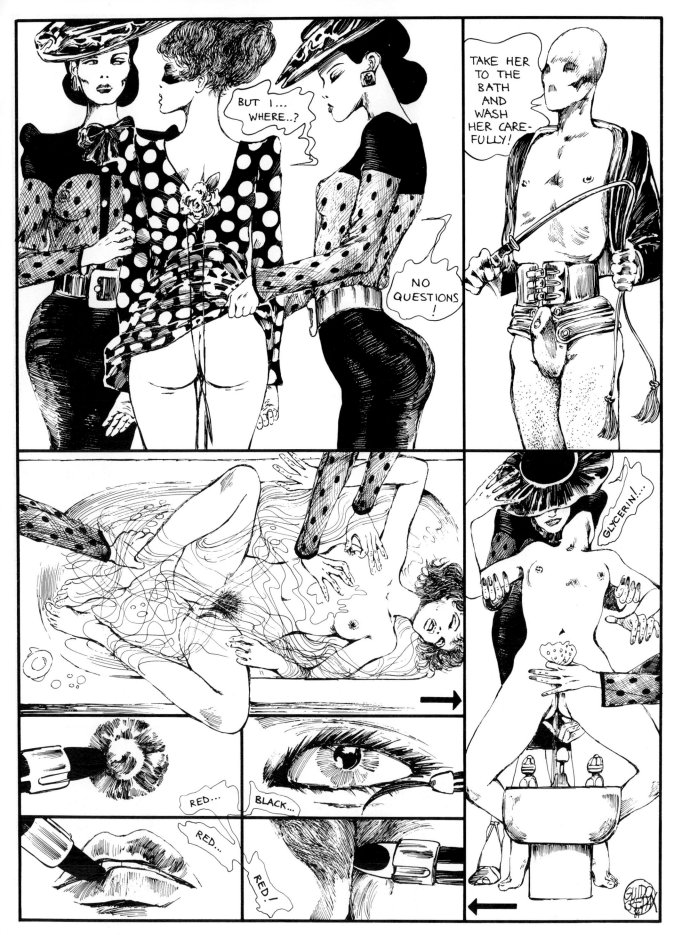

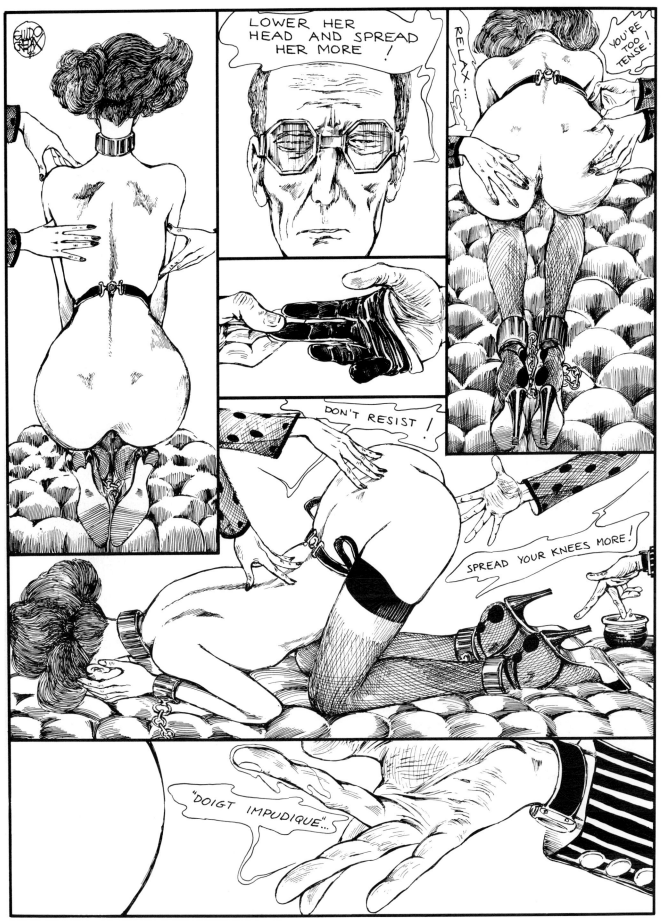

383

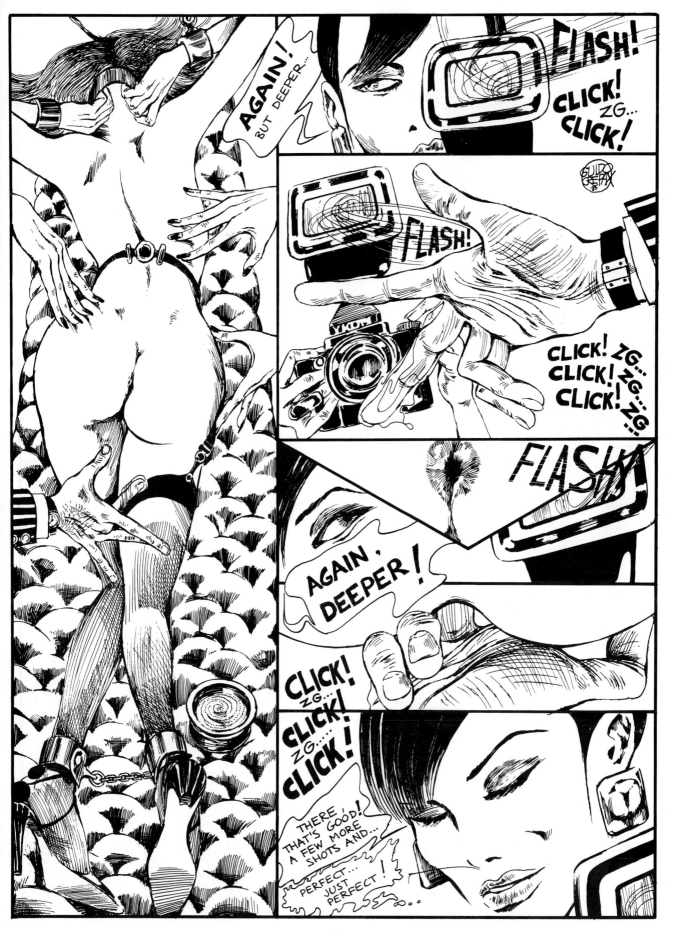

385

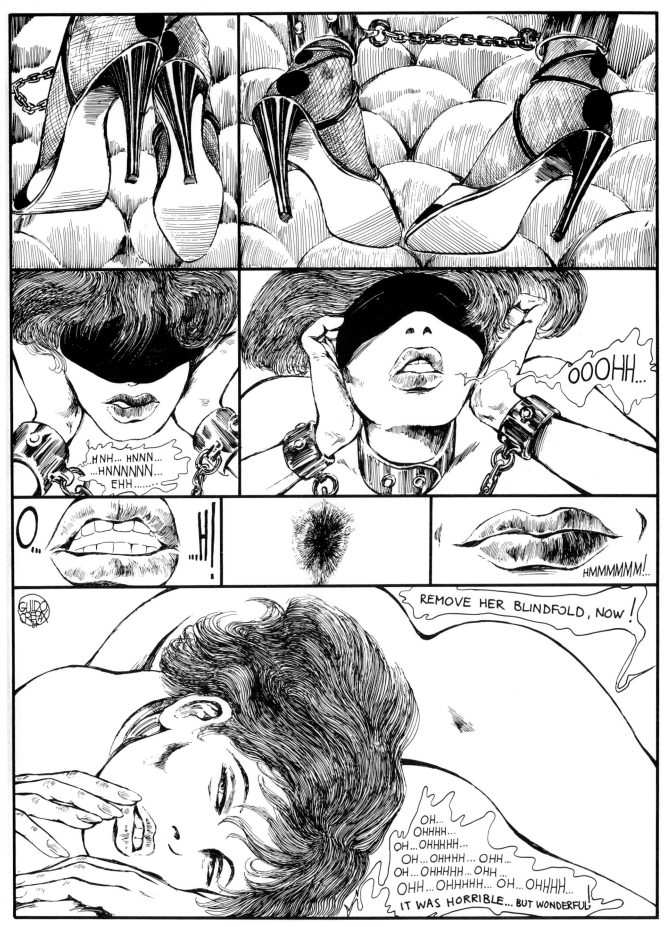

Larry

Dotty

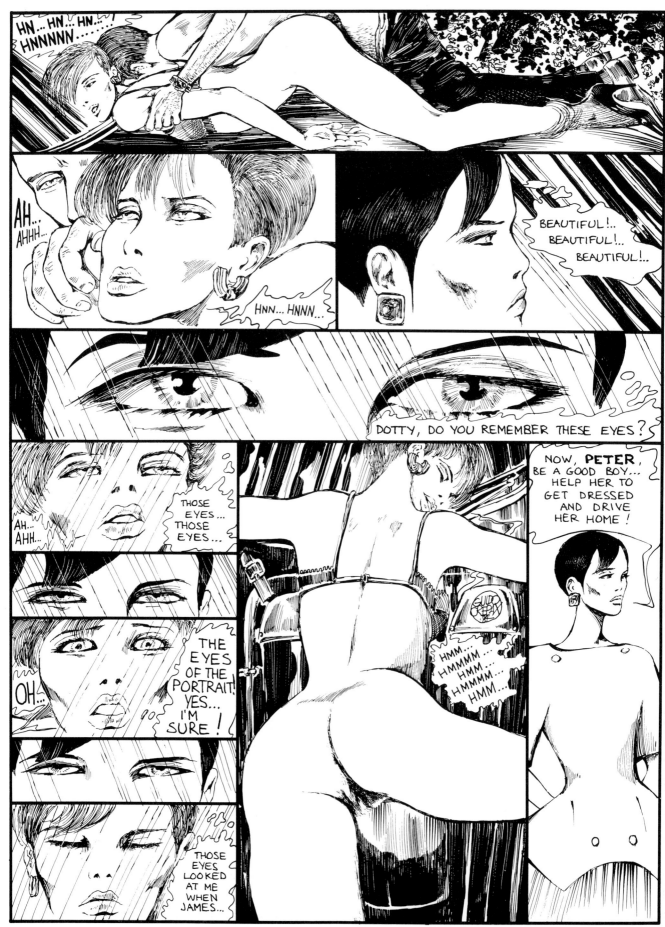

Carol

Confidential Report

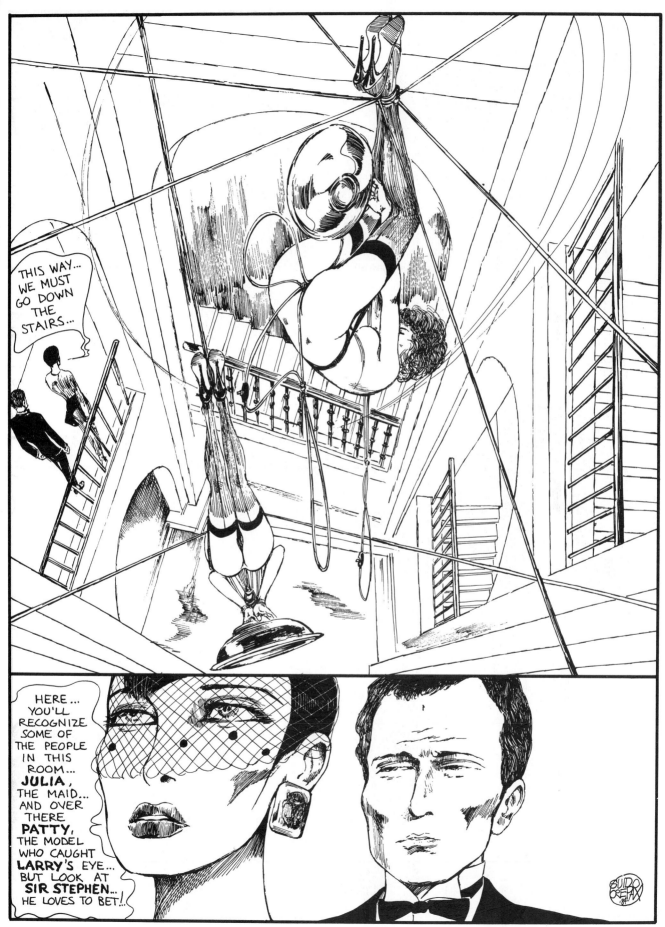

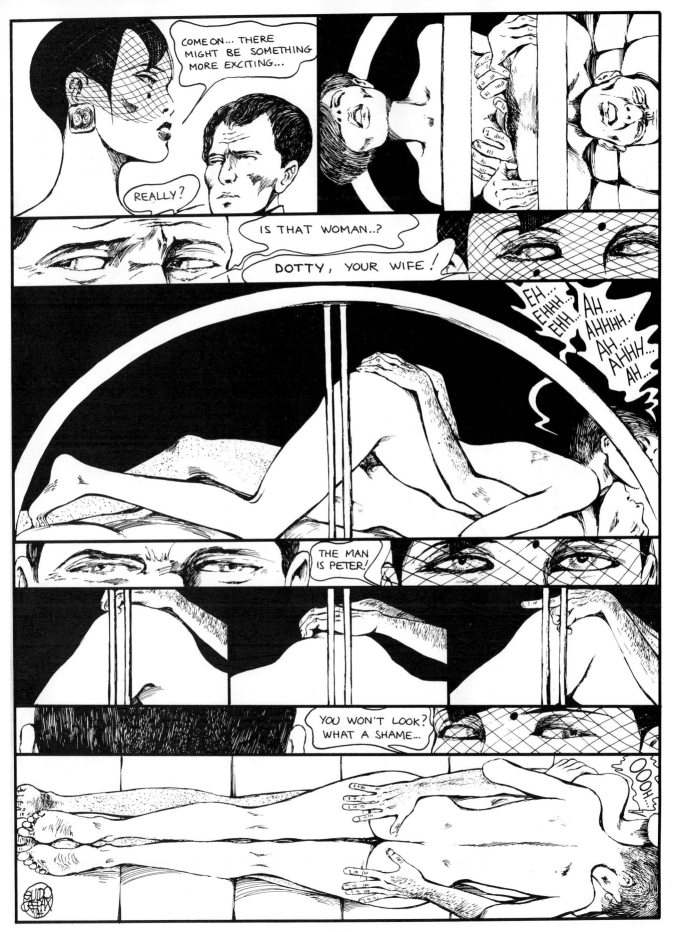

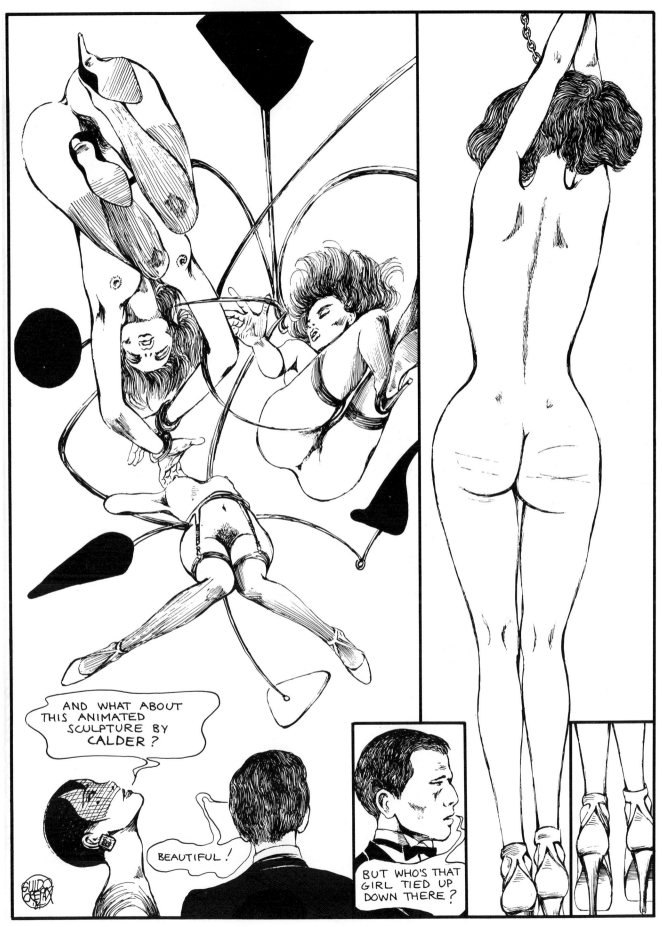

AND WHAT ABOUT THIS ANIMATED SCULPTURE BY CALDER?

BEAUTIFUL!

BUT WHO'S THAT GIRL TIED UP DOWN THERE?

Checkmate

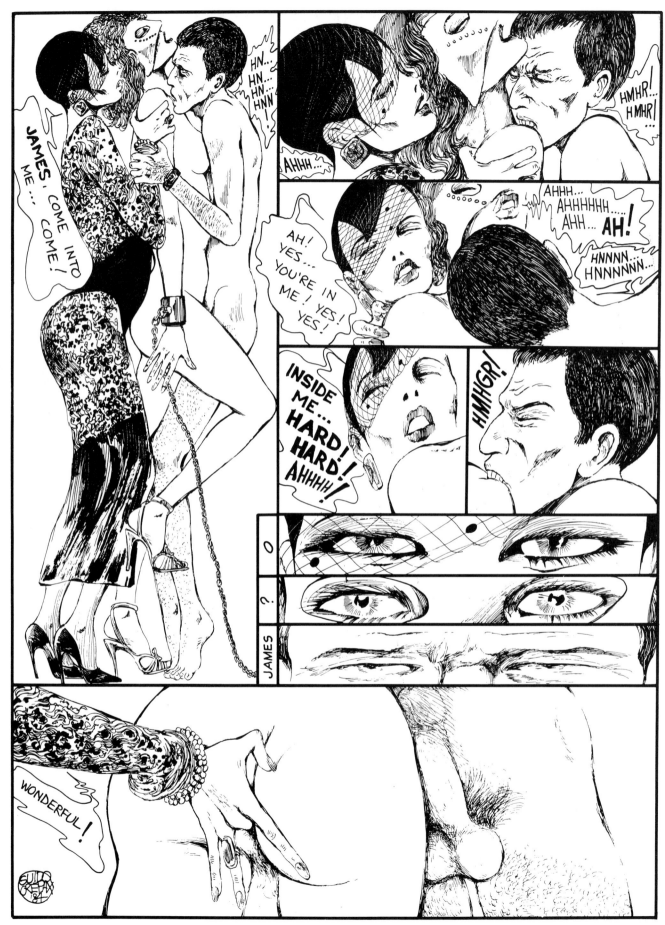

437